American Journal

Christine Montalbetti

AMERICAN JOURNAL

Translated from the French by Jane Kuntz

DALKEY ARCHIVE PRESS

Originally published in French by Éditions P.O.L. as *Journée Americaine* in 2009.

Library of Congress Cataloging-in-Publication Data
Names: Montalbetti, Christine, author. | Kuntz, Jane, translator.
Title: American journal / by Christine Montalbetti ; translated from the French by Jane Kuntz.
Other titles: Journee americaine. English
Description: First Dalkey Archive edition. | Victoria, TX : Dalkey Archive, 2018. | "Originally published French by Editions P.O.L. as Journee Americaine in 2009" -- Verso title page.
Identifiers: LCCN 2009503624 (print) | LCCN 2017057607 (ebook) | ISBN 9781628972535 (pbk. : alk. paper) | ISBN 9782846823500
Subjects: LCSH: Male friendship--Fiction. | United States--Civilization--Fiction. | United States--Social life and customs--21st century--Humor.
Classification: LCC PQ2713.O576 J6813 2018 (ebook) | LCC PQ2713.O576 J68 2009 (print) | DDC 843/.92--dc23
LC record available at https://lccn.loc.gov/2009503624

www.dalkeyarchive.com
Victoria, TX / McLean, IL / Dublin

Dalkey Archive Press publications are, in part, made possible through the support of the University of Houston-Victoria and its programs in creative writing, publishing, and translation.

Printed on permanent/durable acid-free paper

He easily retired the side in the top of the first inning, and in the bottom of the inning the leadoff batter for the Swallows was Dave Hilton, a young American player new to the team. Hilton got a hit down the left field line. The crack of bat meeting ball right on the sweet spot echoed through the stadium. Hilton easily rounded first and pulled up to second. And it was at that exact moment that a thought struck me: You know what? I could try writing a novel.

– Haruki Murakami, *What I Talk About When I Talk About Running* (translated by Philip Gabriel)

There...
on the stone bridge...
over the pond...

waiting for a moon
that never showed,

not all was regret.
[...]

The train whistle moaned
its ballad with the refrain
that reminds us –
journeys begin...
and journeys end...

and that memories
can choose
between beauty
                and loss.

–Nathan Brown

DONOVAN COULD LET MONTHS go by without going to see Tom Lee, but whenever he did, things clicked into place as easy as ever, as if that were the exact day they were meant to meet up again.

Tom Lee would get up out of his wicker chair when he heard the sound of Donovan's car engine, as if he'd been waiting for nothing else, as if that sound filled the empty vessel of his expectation, a perfect fit, like the triumphant insertion of a missing puzzle piece right where it belongs. He'd walk out to the station wagon, unhurried, with the peace of mind that comes when things seem to be happening according to plan. His silhouette would be evenly coated in light, as would his face, whose rounded cheekbones would shine with renewed amiability, while a ray of sunshine would strike the brown of his iris right where his feeling for Donovan was deepest. By the time Tom Lee reached the car, Donovan would have gotten out, and now face to face, they'd give each other a big bear hug in the perfect light.

This is precisely where Donovan is headed right now, straight toward that hug in the perfect light.

He can picture it: their silhouettes, their boots on the sandy ground, the ranch buildings over on the left, the paddock on the right, the mountain range in the background, the eye's only boundary, and overhead, nothing but big sky.

We're exiting the low-density habitat of the suburb where Donovan lives, houses tucked beneath trees, as if crouching anxiously under the spreading branches. Everything seems designed to create shade, there's something snuggly about the architecture, and when you're in the rooms, you're all snuggled up too, in a house that pulls the covers over its head as you curl up against its warm breast.

The morning sunlight arrives at a slant and strikes the leaves with blinding brightness, overexposing the landscape the way morning light does, inviting us to squint and blink to avoid letting too many flying photons corrode the retinas.

Conditions look optimal for driving: we practically have the road to ourselves, nothing between us and the vast sky, just a few puffy clouds gliding by.

We move forward at that laid-back American speed, unhurried, enjoying the comfort of the car's interior, experiencing its exact size and heft from within. The beige upholstery and dash suggest a certain idea of the good life, and once inside this protective enclosure, aren't we experiencing a kind of continuity between this interior and ourselves, as if we'd always belonged here, or you might even say, as if we were gestating inside this beige-carpeted metal shell, sheltered from the outside world, babbling sweetly within its weightless confines.

Once inside, windows up, you can do whatever you like, shout, sing, cry your heart out or laugh yourself silly, but you can most especially do nothing at all, absolutely nothing but keep your foot on the pedal and watch the scenery roll by. There's a very good reason to be staying seated, because at the same time we're exerting zero physical energy, we are nevertheless still moving ahead: action through inaction, which is funny, in a way. You take a load off, relieved of all responsibility, passively forging ahead, all by yourself out there in the American landscape.

Donovan would have trouble recalling the very first time he met Tom Lee. It had to be some point during college, but the exact day, the circumstances, all that's lost in the fog of memory—those mind vapors breathed in and out, ethereal and anaesthetizing, enveloping a moment or event and burying it, fold upon fold.

Friendships are occasionally born at first sight, a primal, unforgettable image so dazzlingly obvious that its mark is indelible. But not all the time. The first encounter doesn't always represent the founding narrative of a friendship, the way it does in iconic love stories, where you're constantly repeating the storyline to yourself, and are therefore less likely to forget it (something reassuring about screening that mental movie in an endless loop), or reliving it with your lovemate (especially early in the relationship, when you ask one another what you were feeling at the time, how you understood things, each articulating how this enchanted moment looked and felt from his or her perspective—and this shared experience goes on to provide the basis for constructing the subsequent chapters of the double-voiced storyline), or retelling it to other people, since the question often comes up in conversation: how did you two meet? And you don't want to be caught off guard, you want to be able to trot out the well-rehearsed legend, the origin story (laundered? streamlined? embellished?) where, the first time your eyes met, a new world of possibilities suddenly opened up. Eventually, you boil down the lovingly fine-tuned, four-hand version of those early times to something much shorter, less detailed, less telltale, something you can serve up to nosy acquaintances who love to hear about other people's love lives, who listen with glistening eyes, as if they were furtively paging through a Harlequin romance.

It's perfectly plausible, I'm the first to admit, that people don't always fall in love the first time they meet, that it takes a change of heart or two, a few extra ingredients, for the magic to work; but either way, it's quite rare, I would think, that those involved would be unable to recall and describe their initial encounter. In fact, you generally find that love's arrows had already hit their mark before you were even aware enough to realize what had happened; and with retrospective analysis, aren't you often delighted to decipher signs that you should have recognized, but which were somehow obliterated by the moment's emotion, the clues that were already present, just under the surface of things, and gave rise to your ensuing love? Those unsuspected meanings that at first escaped your notice, the intricate filigree, the underground river following its course, making its way unattended, only to surface much later, a little silk-wrapped gift laid at your feet by the complexity of experience.

None of this applies to friendship where, quite the opposite, the early stages vanish in favor of a leisurely stratification of the bond.

It's hard to pinpoint the start of a friendship, and the memory of the initial encounter gets clouded by all the subsequent hours spent in one another's company. There's really no point revisiting those earliest times (maybe a few memorable scenes, later ones proving more useful in securing the ties of friendship—"You remember the time when we . . ."), which are often dull and forgettable, lacking the depth of a longer-term relationship that only time can enhance. For a solid friendship is inextricably linked to time, isn't it? Its very substance, the source of that spontaneous comfort you find there, that unshakeable reliability, that permanence, that many-layered treasure whereby every moment spent together (far from weakening the bond, or questioning its validity, allowing those whys to creep in, all those invasive little doubts that undermine your confidence, as is so often the case, unfortunately, with lovers; for you've certainly had the opportunity, as I have, to observe couples dining at a hotel restaurant, sitting in silence across a table, but this silence is not a sign of estrangement, no, look more closely; rather, it means they know each other all too well, as they simmer in the early stages of their poorly negotiated mutual disappointment; all sorts of unpleasant thoughts jostle their way to the surface, producing a hint of spite in the eyes; each has come to realize that their erstwhile enthusiasm and mutual tolerance have given way to dissatisfaction, and they turn this distasteful idea over and over in their minds—and now, the horrid specter of boredom is hovering, even though it is each one's own feelings of personal inadequacy, I believe, that motivates their contempt for the other) strengthens and enriches the affinity. The first encounter has little bearing at all when compared to the strata of accumulated time, that universal binder, the starch, if you will, the thickener that gives friendship its velvety consistency.

The first time Tom's lanky silhouette caught Donovan's eye (i.e., when his retina's rods and cones were activated, transmitting the luminous form to the optic nerve down the predetermined pathway) must have registered somewhere in his memory, but he wouldn't be able to recover that file right now, anyway. He lights up an American Spirit and takes a puff, and maybe the capricious, cloud-like texture of the smoke swirls somehow matches those blurry, out-of-focus images of earlier times.

It all happened gradually, under the radar, they must certainly have crossed paths on several occasions, so that they ended up hanging out on the same grassy quad without ever planning it in advance.

Those were the chrysalis years, there's no more fitting a word, when you went around in that unfinished form of yourself, wondering what kind of creature was evolving inside.

They belonged to that larval stage of youth that clusters on campus lawns, vegetating through their intermediary stage, unsure as to when and how they will reach adulthood. The metamorphosis is slow, and during the process, they prefer the company of their peers, who accept them as they are, at this ill-defined stage of development. They find solace in one another's anxiety that is naturally triggered by this state of transition into the still-unknown self.

The campus buildings and grounds are like bio labs where larvae are kept enclosed to see what form they will take. The specimens are sheltered from the dangers of the outside world, in other words. Once fully formed, they exit the hallowed halls, released into nature as brand-new beings, not realizing that further changes await them. In the meantime, even the lawns seem different from the grass that grows in yards outside the campus perimeter. Their density, the perfection of their crew-cut evenness, and the way the daisies and buttercups stubbornly persist in growing there, with their fatalistic air of victimhood, knowing that they will bloom only to be picked absentmindedly by students who, deep in discussion, will twirl their stems between their fingers as they cogitate. Born to dot the lawns and beds with attractive white and yellow accents, they're also accessories to student reverie, as if, by snapping them like that, or crumpling them in your hand, or twirling them between your fingers, and lowering your gaze to them as they twirl, fragile, helpless, brave and bucolic, pretty, stupid and pointless, you imagine all things that turn, the earth, the whole swirling world, the wheel of time, and all of this is concentrated in one little spinning flower stem, whose movement drives the thought process of the person holding it, ensuring the flow, the forward momentum.

The personalities they brought with them to campus were inchoate at best, and those bodies stretched out on the quad were buzzing inside with random ideas, an unmoored, disjointed vision of things; and each of their gestures and poses only highlighted the incompleteness of their adult personhood, their existence as creatures in the making, rough drafts of who they'll become.

This is why they were kept in isolation by their strait-laced and condescendingly meddling overseers. The teachers and administrators were the lab technicians of this experimental universe, and they brought all their professional know-how to watching over these pupae and cocoons, keeping copious records for each, measuring and noting each stage of their evolution.

Having met at this pupal stage, Donovan and Tom Lee had a sneaking suspicion that they were about to hatch into insects of the same species, and they helped each other evolve toward the form that seemed most appropriate.

And they watched the seasons come and go, the leaves turn yellow and fall, the athletic fields disappear beneath a blanket of snow, and the spring flowers return to field and vale, and to the campus quad where, barefoot and bleary-eyed (their thoughts swirling around sex, literature, and anxiety-inducing ideas as to what the future might hold), they plucked the wildflowers and blades of grass, twirled them, sucked on them, or tickled each other's feet with them, with no other intention than to experience the college green as something made for them, and not the reverse.

And the myriad questions that kept them from enjoying the present moment were on their minds, yes, by the cruel light of day that slammed the lawns and their reclining occupants, and by night as well, as they sat on a bench beneath the midnight-blue canopy, for this is exactly what they did, they sat side by side on their little wooden raft in the middle of an ocean (suddenly calm, enough of a breeze to lightly froth the minuscule waves that shone silver in the moonlight) of possibilities.

These park-bench conversations became a kind of ritual, as they sat with butts up on the backrest, feet on the seat, their topics very different from those discussed by day on the quad, their silences signifying a different sort of reverie.

By day, sprawled out on the grass, nose to the turf or eyes

gazing skyward to check the progress of passing clouds, they'd reflect upon the tenuous, improbable notion of their futures, the enigma of girls, whose every word and deed they examined at length for hidden meanings, for the love message it might be intended to convey. This endless scrutiny lasted well into the afternoon, as the sky above varied its cloud configurations, an indicator of shifts in wind velocity, from gusts to light breezes (high speeds being inevitably associated with freedom, in their minds, while slower ones inspired repose, stationary clouds against a baby-blue sky), filling them with the troubling, thrilling sense of change.

Then, in the evening, from that same uncomfortable park bench perch, leaves rustling in the breeze, the dome of stars wheeling across the sky differently from season to season, the opaque specters of the buildings, ersatz versions of architectures from the ancient world standing guard, they experienced their most intimate moments.

Donovan would sometimes leave to go get his guitar, then return and strum a few tunes for his friend, there in the university night.

He pulled chords out of that sound hole like rabbits out of a hat, and like little bunnies, the miraculous music scampered over the lawn and was gone.

Tom Lee could almost visualize the cycle of those chords emerging and disappearing, obeying Donovan's deft fingering. Maple trees rustled all around them, the lawns seemed to stretch beyond what the eye could see, the buildings stood like victory pennants, and thin, translucent clouds passed like veils over the round, white belly of the moon, now you see it, now you don't, like an exotic dancer in some dark strip bar.

2

LAZINESS IS LIKE WATER: which is what we're mostly made up of, Tom Lee used to say whenever he was accused of being apathetic.

Doing nothing had become an occupation like any other, and the long afternoons they spent out on the quad felt like the very texture of time.

Life continued all around them, and the busy legs of students scissoring their way to and from class along the paved paths did occasionally appear in their peripheral vision, reminding them what a normal academic year should look like. But there was something inappropriate about all that restlessness, something single-mindedly obstinate about locating oneself not quite in the thick of the action—what action would we be talking about here, anyway?—but rather in mere activity, Tom Lee would explain, raising a harmlessly didactic index finger against the backdrop of American lawns, in the fatigue of action without its outcome, without its consequence (that's how I would word it, in any case). I mean, what are all those undergrads trying to achieve, with all that focused energy, deaf and unseeing? They just shuttle themselves around campus, no self-awareness, no critical distance, astonishingly impervious to the supple dance of tree branches that quiver all around them.

Donovan and Tom would sometimes attempt to redeem one of the less stubborn, a quad-walker like the others, but who seemed less herd-minded, more reticent, with something about his gait that signaled he wasn't quite running with the right crowd. They could easily have included him on their park bench in the moonlight and played him a tune or two on the guitar, couldn't they?

But Donovan and Tom approached the matter as statisticians. Happily lounging in the grass, they failed to locate their inner Saint Bernard, unable to muster up the will to mount an intervention aimed at extracting the lost soul from the appalling company he'd fallen in with. Instead, they just lay back and watched the world go by, armchair psychologists casually assessing which ones among the throngs they might have been able to save, pointing them out to each other: what about that one over there? And how about him, the one with his eye on the sky, staring at the vaporous forms of clouds, whose attention span would certainly allow for longer, deeper investigations of the infinite ballet of dust motes caught in a ray of sunshine.

But then, one day, there was Keith Hassanbay.

Keith Hassanbay is a name to remember.

Keith was one of the redeemables, and they often noticed him as they lay in the grass on their stomachs, propped up on their elbows, cheeks resting on their closed fists. They looked more kindly on him with each passing, until they had to admit that his appearance stirred them to wonder.

And when wonder gave way to real interest, they started hanging out together.

Keith was in Cinema Studies, and was doing a PhD on how the death of an actor in the middle of a film shoot requires modifications to the original script. Everyone thought the subject was a bit morbid, but that if you really wanted to think about how stories get cobbled together, it was a neat topic. This kind of situation involved taking a fresh look at the balance among all the characters and how their actions played out in time. He figured you could try to establish a typology of ways to cauterize, so to speak, the gaping hole in the script that the director now had to deal with.

The scriptwriters had very short notice, obviously, to justify a character's sudden disappearance, or to come up with a replacement solution, for example, devising a plot twist involving plastic surgery that would enable them to pursue the same narrative with a different actor. Of course, things get complicated when scenes are shot out of order, which is usually what happens, when, for instance, certain scenes requiring the same set are located chronologically at the beginning and the end, with the intermediary scenes scheduled for a later shoot elsewhere. Reliably stable characters could suddenly get re-scripted as inveterate runaways who'd momentarily disappear from view; classic narrative arcs were suddenly riddled with ellipses, where the viewer was intuitively invited to fill in the blanks, to reconstitute scenes that weren't there. Standard, predictable plotlines would lose their cohesion and became mysterious, leaving viewers with unanswered questions to discuss as they left the theater. Action films got talkier, waxing wordy whenever a character had to explain to another character what had happened, since it was no longer possible to act out the scene. And because not all the solutions to the problem had to do with the script, but also involved tricky camerawork, filmmakers known for close-ups had to make do with long shots where a double would be seen in silhouette, matching as closely as possible that of the deceased star, but whom the audience would recognize as the same character, since he'd be wearing the same blue sweater, the same red hat, or whatever it was he'd been wearing in the previous scene.

Keith Hassanbay would also say—they'd be lying in the grass in a star formation, heads in the center, like an Esther Williams synchronized swimming routine right there on the grass—that the novels you read are like houses, where you can move in and gradually adapt to the particular atmosphere, to the space of each room, to the floor plan and furniture, or if you'd rather, you can rush through the house room by room, opening one door after another, see the whole thing at one go to get an overall idea of the place, to get a sense of the layout, and if the house has won you over, you return to spend more time in this or that room, or in each one in succession, taking all the time you need to get to know the house in all its minute detail, down to the last cubbyhole.

And there they'd be, the three of them sprawled out on the quad, dressed exactly the same, whiling away the hours, alternating pensive silence and intense conversation, processing exactly the kinds of topics that young men do on afternoons like these, one foot in the real world, and one in their own.

When daylight began to fade, they'd get up, knowing that the dinner hour was nigh, a little stiff from the damp ground and lack of movement, but feeling completely fulfilled, and each would then head for his own dorm room, walking his own peculiar walk, on the pretense that he had to pick something up, or drop something off, just long enough to regroup before diving back into the noisy maelstrom of the dining hall.

And then the park bench, with or without Keith.

They could stay there very late into the night, seated side by side, deep in discussion or silence, and when Donovan finally got back to his room, he sometimes had the impression that it was too late to sleep.

Those pre-dawn hours were like the last train: if you miss it, you have to wait until the next morning. So he'd lie there on his back, fully clothed, head resting in the crook of a folded arm, the lights still on, scrutinizing the ceiling for the thousandth time, checking the ever so slow progress of a central crack. It seemed to point to some strange seismic slippage, and never failed to call to mind the great tectonic plates, the horrible prehistoric upheavals, the inconceivable chaos involved in such events, where entire landscapes would crack open and collapse, fold and disappear, as compared to the kinder, gentler idea we get from today's canyons that you can go visit, getting out of your car in your long-sleeved shirts to protect against dangerous UV rays, stretching and taking a few steps in the noonday heat so intense that it feels like a solid.

Then, he would eventually fall asleep, like the cowboys of old, fully dressed.

Donovan takes out another American Spirit, requiring several tries to remove it from among its tightly packed fellow ciggies (a rigid, sky-blue packet featuring an Indian smoking a peace pipe with a little feather hanging off the end), but it finally breaks free, and is now between his lips; he sets it ablaze on the lighter's red-hot coils and draws, and every inhale triggers a memory, as if the cigarette were a little pump that produced puffs of things past.

Maybe the first time Donovan and Tom Lee met, now that I think of it, was at the football stadium. The nebulous origins of that friendship must have drawn on the ambiguous festivities of those games, when the Oklahoma Sooners were playing the Colorado Buffaloes, the players all suited up in their pads and helmets and face masks, running back and forth under the glare of stadium lights.

You know what it's like at a college football stadium, right? The students are there in the stands, watching, cheering, having a good time, talking about other things, letting their thoughts wander sometimes, in a kind of accordion rhythm alternating tension and release. But the real winners, in my view, are the mosquitoes.

3

FOR AN OKLAHOMA MOSQUITO, the fall football schedule means king-size festivities, and they must prepare all year for this season, which lasts about ten weeks, right up to when they decamp for the winter.

No need to wander pathetically in gardens and patios, following the vague trace of carbon dioxide in the air, in search of a tear in a screen through which to enter a sleeping household. A stadium full of fans represents tons of available flesh, conveniently installed in parallel rows of bleachers, exposed unshielded to the American night.

And there's the kickoff. Our little fifteen-ounce ball grows heavier with speed, and knowing that, it flies above the stadium in a predictable arc whose trajectory is followed by hundreds of pairs of eyes. Once it reaches its apogee, it starts its descent, aiming for the arms of a kickoff returner who's ready and waiting downfield, who has trained to absorb the shock, and having caught the ball, sets off running as if nothing in the world mattered.

Like him, the quarterback also takes his role to heart, surrounded by his linemen who form a mobile rampart of bodyguards, cutting a path for him, watch out, they're on the move now, slicing through the defense, that's what they're out there for, and when they meet resistance, they push, while the other side pushes right back, big torsos with a job to do, shamelessly violent, no latitude for qualms, apparently.

Yes, but he has to throw a pass at some point, not just hog the ball the whole time, though now it looks like he's going to try to run it through; brain's on fire under that helmet, eyes scanning the scene, assessing the situation, he fakes to the right, then pivots, well-worn strategies that still work, not sure how come they still work, no time to stop and think about it with the defensive line bearing down and the clock ticking, can't fall back on the same old plays, the memorized formations, and there's a wide receiver who's giving you some authoritative distress signals that seem to be saying what the fuck are you doing, are you going to pass it or what, and he does look to be in position, doesn't he? Overhead, the vast black sky, and underfoot, this rectangle of tart green grass is all you can see, but you still haven't made up your helmeted mind, between yielding to the wide receiver's pressure to throw, and your own desire to try for the down on your own, and right at that instant, you start to wonder about yourself, how you got there, everything that conspired for you to be the one clutching a football to your chest. But you're brought back from this split-second of self-scrutiny in the frenzy of action, in the heat of the game and the fear of defeat, when two powerful arms grab you around the legs, making any further yardage impossible, and with the ball still in your possession, you feel the turf moving toward you and you're down, you fumble the ball in the process, the ground hits you smack in the face, and that's all, the clock stops, get up, it's starting all over again.

The defense lines up again, drawn like a curtain, everyone knows what to do, the opposing quarterback sets up the play, and snap. He hesitates, should he pass to the wide receiver, who's open and waiting, or to that other one way downfield, whose touchdown sprints are history-making, whatever the case, even while hesitating, he's still inching forward; when crunch time comes, he'll decide. And he decides, since everything happens so fast, of course. It's to the wide receiver, here, see what you can do with it, and on it goes, the game plays itself out beneath those big American skies, those wide-open spaces.

Our invisible little flying critters are sharing that same space and sky, wings humming, performing figure-eights in the cooling air, zigzagging to dodge the occasional swat, happy hunters.

Even though it's autumn, and they know they'll soon have to find someplace to spend the winter, our bloodsucking friends are enjoying the feast, and they're always at their very best after dark. Under the blazing stadium lights, against the blackness of night and the chiaroscuro of the playing field, they're just happy to be alive and thriving. Armies of these dipterans with their invasive labrum are making reconnaissance flights above the bleachers. The collection of bodies below, it has to be said, looks to them like an all-you-can-eat buffet, they hardly know where to begin as they fly dizzily about, giddy to the point of nausea almost, but they're so happy.

Of course, there are always a few tough customers who've come coated in citronella, but their proportion is statistically insignificant; overall, this is a pretty approachable crowd. And then there are those who fell for those insect repellent bracelets you can buy in all kinds of colors, green, fuchsia, electric blue, but they don't work at all, they're just fashion statements, wrist candy or whatnot (if you want to know the truth, geranium is the only thing that really does the job, but can you imagine every fan showing up at the stadium with a potted geranium on his knees?), and the mosquitoes stuff their guts just the same, bracelet or no bracelet, no surprise there.

They take all the time they need to choose a target; look, there's an easy one, how about that bald head right over there, all those appetizing vessels exposed and available, O how delightfully vulnerable they are, it brings a tear to the eye. That helpless, white roundness against the night sky, under the stadium lights that bounce off it like a dead planet in the path of some distant star's rays. It feels like a moon landing to the mosquitoes. One particularly anthropophilic specimen, newly arrived on the bald planet, pauses a moment to reflect on the skull's owner who will be going back home in a little while to his house beneath the shade trees, greeted by his loyal dog that has spent the entire evening sprawled on its oversized doggy cushion, performing its guard duties with a kind of vigilant indolence, though its heart is plagued, as always, by the nagging suspicion—you can't teach an old dog new tricks—that this time, its master will not return.

The house must be screened in, like all houses around here, mesh rectangles that click into place on all windows and screen doors. So you can only imagine, dear friends, the long and difficult search for a chink in that armor, a worn spot, any warped area that has pulled away from the frame, enabling the little winged creatures free entry onto the premises to commit their evil deeds.

Our mosquito is picturing in full Technicolor the happiness that awaits as it finally springs into action. Here's how you do it: you station at just the right distance from your desired target (you have built-in stabilizers), you choose an axis, and down you go to plant your rostrum in the epidermis. Within seconds, you've injected the victim with a little homemade anesthesia, so that he feels nothing on contact, and while you're at it, with an anti-coagulant: *voilà*, everything's ready now for the draw. Like sucking through a straw, you take it in, lucky to have such extensible abdominal membranes that allow you to stretch and fill with the divine nectar, whose endless range of subtle flavors—and this is a homage to your victims—you've yet to fully explore.

Let's not kid ourselves, this puncture is soon going to cause the bald man's scalp no end of grief. The numbing effect can last only so long, and once he's in bed, under the covers in the humid autumnal night (still too early to switch on the central heat), probably replaying some highlights of the game as he gets comfortable, our pre-sleeper reaches his hand to his head, unconsciously at first, to scratch the site of the bite, but then, fully aware of the itch-inducing inflammation, will scratch more vigorously, as he mumbles a string of unflattering epithets with regard to our little critters and their insatiable appetite. In this house he thought sealed securely against such invaders, he'll try to retreat into the swampy world of dreams, all the while scratching the now reddened area, hoping to calm the irritation when he's actually making it worse.

Our miniature vampires still have blood on their probes as they leave in search of their next victim. Meanwhile, a halfback plowing downfield, cleats tearing up the turf, gets tackled, fumbles, loses possession, the ball gets picked up by an opposing lineman, the ref whistles the turnover, and it goes on like that, another receiver makes a catch and puts a knee to the ground, etc., while the flesh of the hale and hearty fans in the stands continues to furnish an inexhaustible supply of nutrition in the cooling night air.

How many times did Tom and Donovan sit in those stadium bleachers, eyes riveted on the bulked-up bodies that fought over possession of the pigskin with such impressive energy (you can say whatever you want, but twenty-two guys whose whole world depends on an oval-shaped leather ball, there's something amazing and mind-blowing about that, really makes you think, proclaimed Mike). The white-stripe yard lines set against the grass shining beneath the floodlights that exalt the surreal green, and since most of the action takes place midfield, the graceful goalposts at either end have to wait their turn. In the background, the water tower looks almost fake, a fat metallic bulb on stilts, a curious silhouette against the empty sky.

Look at those distorted forms stuffed into all that padded gear, as they seem to shuffle around a little before crashing into each other (the defensive linemen divvy up the work, there are never enough of them when it comes to holding back the opposing team who, let's face it, are giving our guys a hard time out there; no, this is not a piece of cake, you have to take some hits if you want to stop them, throw yourself into it, forget your mother and father and plunge into the fray, which is exactly what they do), their exaggeratedly wide shoulders making them look like a herd of stampeding bison tearing up the grassy plain.

These guys' bodies are protected like crazy, there's a whole ritual to the pre-game swaddling.

You want to try it out, just to see? Suit up in one of those uniforms? To start, you lay out your first layer, like a winding cloth to wrap a mummy, but not a full-body wrap, just a strip here, a strip there, giving precedence to the joints: base of the thumb, ankles, and don't forget the knees, of course, using your basic Ace bandage, a practical, adaptable material, light and easy to handle.

Let's keep going. You then apply a plastic corset to your ribs, held in place by a pair of wide suspenders (everything in varying shades of white, so as not to clash with the Ace bandages).

All right, now for the elbow pads, thigh and butt guards, tailbone protector, tell me if I'm going too fast, and knee pads, a mixture of plastic and foam that you insert into specially designed pockets in your pants.

But wait, there's more. You now put on your shoulder pads (this is the most impressive feature, the one that makes you look like a buffalo). The foam contents are treated with an anti-bacterial substance, since a player is likely to be doing quite a bit of sweating out there on the field, not that anyone holds that against him, but they'd prefer that the foam be treated to avoid the mold and mildew that could proliferate in the dark dampness of a football uniform. You lace up easily, thanks to laces located conveniently right below the sternum, and then someone helps you into your jersey, which goes over everything else.

At this point, all that's left are your socks and cleats, and you're ready, go have a look in the mirror.

You exit the locker room, running to warm up, and you spill out onto the field. You put on your helmet, which you've been holding under one arm (the helmet is also heavy-duty, hard plastic outside, air vents, generously lined inside with individual sections of foam padding, adorned with a more or less flattering face mask composed of plastic-coated metal bars, whose grillwork can vary according to what position you play, and attached to all that, a chin strap. Every player gets his own cutom-made mouth guard, molded to each one's jaw and teeth. Some players even have polycarbonate visors, steam-proofed to avoid the inconvenience of having your vision blurred by your own breathing, which would be a real shame). And you let it all wash over you, the noise from the stands, the humid, sweaty atmosphere, the first signs of autumn in the air. The sound of your own footsteps is absorbed by the grass and the foam-lined helmet, you look mean, your eyes sharpen, but at the same time, you feel so cushioned, not an unpleasant feeling at all, you're at once vigilant and trusting, you're about to plunge into a very special time, suspended and yet accelerated, as the time of adventure always is.

Immersed into this very special texture of time, you start to move, a supersized, augmented body, you're an alien, a steel reinforced animal, all plastic and nylon, with a little bit of flesh vibrating somewhere inside.

To that flesh, our bloodthirsty insect friends shouldn't expect to gain easy access. The hurly-burly of those twenty-two bodies in action gives them scant opportunity. They're moving too fast, too unpredictably for you to land and pump from that slippery skin covered in so much protective gear as to make the job impossible. No, you won't be setting any records with these guys. You might think it possible to somehow slip in between the helmet and the face mask, but frankly, I wouldn't advise it: you risk getting trapped inside, stuck in a pearl of sweat, where you'd expire in darkness while you look out through the mask and see the playing field waver as the runner dashes to first down under the blinding stadium lights.

Still, if you know how to go about it, there are plenty of other occasions out there on the field.

The second-string bench warmers look like sitting ducks, over there on the sidelines, not doing much, except watching the A-list play. Looks like just the thing we're after, and what a win for us if we can score a bite off one of them and get away with a gut-full of their blood, flying over the stadium secure in the knowledge that we're not just any old mosquitoes. Though I have to admit that they're all so jittery to get out there and play, so tight and focused on the moment, that they contract their muscles in a way that makes it hard for us to perform that first puncture. So I guess we could also keep our distance and look down on them with an air of *I wouldn't stoop to that*, as if to say that we've got better things to do.

After that, it's a matter of taste. You've got your referees, seven in all, scattered evenly around the field, wearing striped polo shirts and white trousers, but it's not their fashion statement that's at issue here. Their ball caps fit too tightly, while their exposed arms, neck, and cheeks hold out a certain potential. The top ref makes hand signals when necessary, and he's got dozens to choose from. He'll run through quite a few: arms raised, arms down—my personal favorite is the illegal pass: facing the press box, top of the right hand pressed flat against the lower back, and I also like the incomplete forward pass, where he crosses his arms over his chest at shoulder height. But all of them are fun to watch.

The refs have to keep their eyes glued to the action, this isn't the time to get distracted. The optic nerve sends high-speed information packets that need to be processed immediately (an fMRI would show a high activity level in certain cortical areas), and need I mention that there is no room for even the glimmer of a question as to the presence of mosquitoes in the vicinity. No, their undivided attention is devoted to spotting foul play, to watching who's moving where, to registering and understanding all the stats, they've got plenty to think about as it is. Which is why we can allow for a nosedive into their epidermis, for what it's worth.

The most delicious are the majorettes, though. Ah, the majorettes! Those bare legs, what a feast, and so easy to find a tasty vein right beneath such delicate skin, so fine, so yielding to the puncture, still fragrant from their cherry and pear-scented shower gel, with just a hint of salt brought on by all that strenuous dancing.

Or, instead of hanging out on the gridiron, you could also go all the way up to the press box where all the journalists and announcers sit.

Headphones over their ears (don't even think about going for the earlobe, you'll never make it), commentators do the play-by-play, and you can't tell how much personal history each one brings to the job. They go wild over a pass, exalt over a first down, or fret over missed opportunities, their eyes stuck like magnets to the field whose green glows electric under the lights. But isn't there something in their voice, despite their level of involvement in the game as witnessed by the force of their delivery, some vocal inflection that conveys a sense of their private self that they've had to set aside for the duration of this sports event? It's hard to know how much their tone of voice can say about personal concerns, mental states, or unresolved issues, all of which have nothing to do with their attitude toward the outcome of the game or the injuries sustained by this or that player—Oh man!, it looks like he's taken a bad hit—but which have everything to do with entire chapters of their life that get folded and put away as soon as the microphone is turned on, since the requirements of the profession make no allowance for all that; and yet those personal issues manage to redeploy and lift into the evening breeze, just a rustle of the vocal chords that involuntarily communicates a secret emotion.

If Colorado is playing tonight, you'll see Ralphie over there, off to the side, hello old girl, waiting patiently in a small paddock hardly larger than she is.

Who is Ralphie? Well, she's a live bison, mascot of the Colorado Buffaloes (every team needs one, right?) that gets released and paraded around the field by a group of handlers; poor creature has no idea what this performance is all about, but carries out her duty with remarkable sangfroid, though never ceasing to wonder why she's there, at this particular moment, in front of a packed stadium.

The Ralphie you see there isn't the original, since there have been many successors over the years, each bearing its dynastic number. At the time of this writing (look, it's snowing, for once, on the streets of Paris, outside my window), I can only speak for Ralphie V, a frisky female with no more insight than her predecessors as to the reasons she gets displayed like that before the overflow crowd, but she's more or less submissive, eyes on the freshly mowed grass that looks pretty pathetic compared to the meadow where they have her graze, no, nothing very appetizing here, she gallops forward without salivating amid the deafening cheers, it's unpleasant but she'll get through it all right, as she always does.

The rest of the time, I guess you could say there's not a bison around that's as pampered as this one. Luxury ranch, great view of the mountains, all the fodder she can eat, unlimited pasture,

a buffet of alfalfa and oats, you could do a whole lot worse than
grazing your brains out under the big Colorado skies.

The first Ralphie, inaugurating the series in the mid-sixties,
officiated for a good dozen years, something you wouldn't
necessarily know about, I would guess, before stepping down
in favor of Ralphie II, who didn't last quite as long, and was
forced out by Ralphie III, who, it turned out, was still a little
young. But she did perform adequately, except for one slapstick
incident when she broke free from her handlers; those things
can happen, and have happened, over the long history of the
Ralphies.

The fourth of the dynasty came to her title at the right age.
A coyote had nearly killed her when she was still a young calf,
and one wonders whether she was psychologically scarred by
the episode. Not at all unlikely. Her stadium career was more
eventful than the others', her personality more unstable, her
reactions less predictable. With those sullen looks of a bison
who's seen it all, but still has a few tricks up her sleeve, she
was less docile, which demanded extra focus on the part of
her very nervous handlers who were understandably worried
that she would take advantage of her overwhelmingly superior
strength and break free to go head-butt someone, let's see, what
might you enjoy, maybe that line of smiley cheerleaders over
there, with their inane high-kicking and swirly short skirts,
knocking two over and goring another, not a pretty picture,
definitively discrediting the line of Ralphies, the pride of every
citizen of Boulder, Colorado. Something about that early trauma
made people feel protective of her, I guess, and her occasional
escapades were simply her way of struggling with the horrible
memory that would return to haunt her, though they left a
certain bitterness in the hearts of the good folks of Boulder.

Our Ralphie V is more easygoing, an uneventful upbringing,
nothing noteworthy in her biography, we're delighted for her.

Born in 2006 and full of promise, even though one of her horns is slightly damaged (several versions of how that happened are in circulation). Truth be told, she does have a few pranks to her credit, but you can chalk those up to youthful insouciance, nothing to write home about.

The inhabitants of Colorado towns love it when Ralphie passes by in her pickup truck, I can tell you that for sure. They rush to their windows, Look there's Ralphie, and soon the whole household is trying to get a glimpse, good old Ralphie, everyone's always happy to see her behind the metal bars of that truck, or supporting the home team at games, they feel a wave of affection for her every time that truck passes, with her name in big gold letters on the side, Hey, there she goes, it's Ralphie.

Just as your Ralphie predecessors did, you forge your own idea of what life's all about, accepting the shabby paddock at the stadium, the skimpy pickup truck you have to ride in, the ludicrous laps around the football field to the roaring cheers of the crowd, especially at halftime (they've gotten all warmed up by then, up there in the bleachers), because there's also the air out there on the prairie, where they come and brush you down, talk to you in a language you don't understand but which sounds friendly and admiring—these are great moments of happiness, out there beneath the open sky, with everything you need right at hand.

As for the Oklahoma team, ours that is, it's something else altogether: what you see at the beginning of each half is a small-scale covered wagon, painted in school colors, pulled by two rugged-looking, snow-white ponies, their minds a blank behind their blinders, and driven by a guy standing, reins in hand, eyes on the field in front of him, while some beauty queen or other sits next to him, smiling and waving to the crowd, bare-armed.

This kitschy paraphernalia is supposed to replicate the arrival of the settlers, folklore for the sports field, conjuring up some warped western nostalgia, revisited and reprocessed into a cleaned-up, palatable version, a page of American history impossible to turn.

This is the mascot of the Sooners, a reference to the great land rush, to those who arrived sooner than others to stake their claim, but today, it's just a source of chauvinist pride: the Sooner, the Better.

The clear advantage of this mascot over the Ralphies is that a Conestoga wagon can have no second thoughts as its wheels turn obediently on their axles, experiencing no pleasure or pain. The assemblage of planks and canvas, hinges and dowels, neither aches nor moans, just dashes around the field in the absence of any self-awareness or emotion, indifferent to the floodlights or the noisy strangeness of the scene.

But let's get back to our mosquitoes: at this point, out on the playing field, the Sooners are still clasping that nearly weightless ovoid object as if nothing in the world were more important, that leather egg they want to keep all to themselves, defend from the enemy like furious, heroic mother hens, exhausting themselves before the cheering crowd.

While the players keep acting out the timeless desire to keep things for oneself, the learned behavior of sharing only with people you know, and the atavistic urge to steal what the adversary possesses, the mosquitoes resume their flight pattern around the stadium, but hasn't something in them changed? Has a new sensation replaced their earlier unmitigated enthusiasm, when they flitted about carefree, heedless of what tomorrow might bring?

Earlier, they were basking in the warm glow of impunity, in the undisturbed happiness that opulence alone can afford, and now, all of a sudden, they're not in such great shape. Something insidious has seeped into their souls, and the ribbed wings they deployed with such vim only moments ago now feel heavy and limp, like sails that have taken on water.

And there's a reason for this: the same profusion that made them so giddy has now exhausted them. They no longer know what to do with so many choices.

Our little critters are having trouble exercising their free will, and they're thinking that recent events must have stirred up some murky, unconscious reason for this new indecisiveness, circumstances they'd thought buried and forgotten but that have resurfaced to undermine their will, turning them into mindless, irresolute creatures. Things that go back to their childhood, because it's not at all the same thing if your mother deposited the egg from which you hatched on the surface of a cute little pond (where inverted images of surrounding trees were mirrored against a blazing blue sky), or on the banks of some river (where the reflected landscape gets blurred), or—what were those mothers thinking—in rainwater collecting in a discarded truck tire, or in the effluvia of a sewer pipe, or any other insalubrious location where your mother had the poor judgment to drop you off, believing that mere moisture (and subsequent proteins) would be enough to nourish the larva that you would become in a dozen or so hours; for she doesn't think for a moment, the poor dear, that the place where you open your eyes for the first time could possibly count for anything in later life.

Its mother, whom, might I add, it has never seen, who just did what she had to do, when it came to egg-laying and all, but who, after leaving you on your own, like a mother abandoning her child on the steps of a church, hit the road again, the way the proverbial cowboy does, moving on, a trail of tear-stained regrets in his wake.

So it's not impossible that our reluctant mosquitoes, befuddled by their own ineptitude, started thinking back to those puddles of their birth, to their orphan journey into the world (whether in a magnificent landscape or the bottom of some gutter), since, one way or the other, you had to learn how to get along on your own without parental help, and how those early days affected their self-image and the way they relate to others, and which, in the long run, have rendered them so incapable when it comes to decision-making. We're ruminating on all that while the frenzied fans cheer on the players, increasingly excited as the clock counts down the final minutes, and we fret over our unresolved issues that still tie our guts up in knots and spoil our enjoyment of all the available flesh on offer, we can be really stupid sometimes.

All of that by way of saying that, yes, Donovan and Tom did spend a lot of time in the bleachers attending football games, just like the other undergrads did, side by side, sharing in the suspense inherent in the sport, exclaiming at the beauty of a block or pass amid the scramble and click of colliding helmets that glint and dart under the stadium lights, helmets housing stubbornly bellicose thoughts, all intent upon a single goal: to take possession of that seemingly insignificant fifteen-ounce prize, the coveted pigskin.

They were there for the beauty of the game, no doubt, but also because the girls went, and it was so wonderful to watch them follow the action, all tense and excited, but equally wonderful when they'd get bored with the game and begin looking around, and sometimes, your eyes would meet theirs, but often you could tell by their look that they had retreated into some interior world, where God only knows what was going on.

4

IF YOU COULD MANAGE to catch some girl's eye several times in a row during a football game, you could maybe hope for a date later the same week, and I'll tell you where you'd take her: out to a field full of dips and mounds, where there's a little creek with a bridge that used to serve as a backdrop for Renaissance fairs—you can still see what remains of a drawbridge, grandiose but serving no purpose—and is now completely abandoned, between the road and the train tracks, with the stadium in the distance, not in use that evening, but still a reminder of the day you met, when it all started.

You'd wait until sundown, then walk out, side by side through the uneven grass (sometimes she'd grab your arm to keep from twisting an ankle on the irregular terrain in poor visibility). First, you'd go to the duck pond, where one of two things would happen: either you'd head for the little bridge, and after saying a couple things about how it had been used, without taking the girl's hand, to keep the suspense alive, you'd walk over to it; or you'd sit down right there by the duck pond on the stone bench. All around, the cypress tree roots jut out of the ground, form knotty growths that rise like stalagmites, their jagged crests looking oddly like some range in the Rockies, a scale model of mountainous terrain. Further off, the spindly silhouette of the water tower next to the placid stadium building, painted white with a beam of red light shining on it, all looking unreal against the dense dark sky. You could hear cars passing on the nearby road and see their headlights as you sat there, mingling the experience of the pond, the deep sky, and the grassy knolls with distant movement of car traffic—and why not get poetic about it—that lit up the ribbon of roadway with uneven, unpredictable glitter.

At your back were the train tracks, used by both passenger trains and the endless strings of freight cars, both of which sounded that powerfully evocative whistle that you can still hear long after the train has passed, piercing the boundless landscape uninterrupted until it reaches your eardrums and revives in your ancestral memory the legendary stories of how the railroad built the West. It happens every time, those whistles never fail to stir up something in your unconscious, when you're busy doing something else, and suddenly, the sound reaches your ears: tales of the Far West, the laying of the rails, the blueprints unrolled across the desks of decision-makers, the dubious deals transacted among men in three-piece suits, all those laborers at work on the dusty land. And as the good folk of Oklahoma drift off to sleep under the covers, those distant, lonesome midnight whistles drill into their heads the narrative of their ancestors who built railroads, their sweat and can-do spirit, the lives that went into this vast construction, and their dreams fill with gangs of workers digging up the sandy soil, the enormous debt they owe these brave forebears, as they slumber in their cozy rooms in their hyper-organized world.

Still, that was always the cue to kiss the girl, the piercing stridence of the train whistle that ripped through the landscape, to which was added the quacking of disputatious ducks bickering over something or other (one sharp quack at a rival would sum up one duck's opinion of another, a malicious but well-deserved outburst), or the incessant croaking of frogs, the bucolic music of the pond mixing with all the rest, the traffic, the view of the stadium, everything melded into a single experience, vegetable and mineral, motors and materials, a range of sound and light, to form a dense, complex place that lent itself so well to the meeting of lips—and tongues, too, just a little, the soft, warm volume of tongues that reached and retracted, boldly or timidly, under the great vault of American sky.

I'm telling you all this from experience (never let it be said that I didn't do my research), because I was one of the girls who got kissed in that place. It was at a later age, during a recent trip, but it was great, all that dark green grass at night, the car parked down below, the headlights of passing vehicles, the little bench near the pond, the bridge (it was on the bridge for me) where you walk halfway and stop, you look each other in the eyes, not too long, to see if you're in agreement here, but also allow for the possibility that nothing will happen while keeping alive the hope that something will happen, be patient, here we go, getting closer, and there it is, the embrace, I highly recommend it, out there overlooking the little creek flowing below, a thin rivulet, hardly a creek at all, it's more like the idea of a creek, to join lips, then tongues, and feel the other's body through their clothing, with the stadium in the background, softly lit, and the powerful whistle of the train as it rumbles past, shaking the ground, filling the sound-space, I was having a great time, and as always, that endless skyway stretching forever over the Oklahoma flatlands; thank you, I won't forget (anyway, it's in the book now).

These same flatlands that Donovan is driving across, eating up the miles like a retractable measuring tape, yes, it was like being inside the metal sheath of a measuring tape, sucking up the ribbon of blacktop that looks like some unstoppable mechanism is causing it to enter from under the carriage.

Trees border the road, small round ones at first, casting sharp shadows, each one planted, it seems, in the middle of a gray-tinted circle. Then others, more wind-blown, leafier and more massive.

Then the birches.

Then two or three houses with tall trash cans out by the road—the whole roadside timeline that shows how people here live, how they raise livestock and kids, how they plant and how they abandon, and how they weave their network of unapparent relationships (not a single living human in sight since he hit the road).

He passes a tank truck, finally.

He glides past a windowless corrugated iron building, displaying the word *Karaoke*, a glassy pond reflects the sky, a luminous area in the matte flatland, some vineyards, a gas station displaying its giant yellow half-shell.

On the outskirts of the campus, just across the way from one of the brick gates marking the school's perimeter, there were a few restaurants, some of which had outdoor seating where, weather permitting, you could sit under the trees that were decorated with fine strings of microscopic, colorless electric lights wound around the trunks, creating tiny points of light against the rough bark. And there, munching on chicken sandwiches or a serving of nachos—for those not in the know, the melted cheese, all stringy and elastic, breaks into a dozen threads with each bite, and you manage however you can—Tom would talk to whoever was listening about how a stroke of paint made by a master Japanese potter on a teacup constitutes the tiny defect that (they say) makes the whole so beautiful and keeps things interesting. That we're each a little defective in some way, but out of that flaw springs our beauty, to a certain degree, he would explain, interrupted by that hoarse, breathy laugh of his that punctuated the otherwise fluid diction of his sentences like the sound of (hard to imagine anything more similar) pebbles in a fast-running stream.

This was the *wabi-sabi* aesthetic that Tom would trot out whenever needed.

It provided him with a convenient conversation topic out there on the restaurant patio in the creamy depths of the Oklahoma night. He'd use it to show off in front of girls, deploying his ideas like wings, letting the air resound with their meaning, yes, because defects, don't you see, are not something hideous to be hidden away, because they're what make us alive. Alive, and therefore, desirable.

His theory applied to just about anything, such as a pimple on the face, no cause for concern anymore, because its presence, there next to the eyebrow, was a very moving sight, or the one near your mouth that seemed inevitably to attract attention to that part of your face and arouse the urge for a kiss. A facial blemish, expounded Tom, not only set off the beauty of the rest, but it contributed to that beauty, stirred up emotions, aroused desire; it was the thin fissure through which you present yourself to the other, your fragile, vulnerable, and eminently worthy self, to be held in the arms of the other, who seeks to surround you, to protect you from all that, to allay your fears, don't worry, it's nothing at all, that silly old pimple, and you'll be kissed all the better, all the more tenderly, than if you had presented a face smoothed over with makeup whose matte texture unthinkingly absorbs the emotion, congeals it in the flesh-colored paste, and leaves it for dead.

And this holds true for all feelings of inadequacy, whenever you believe you've failed to meet some standard, and shamefaced, you slink away from the situation at the first opportunity. We were imperfect, but that's precisely what made us lovable, Tom would conclude, and he'd present himself to the girl in all his imperfectness, which he'd wear like medals that would sparkle in the moonlight that must have been shining on the restaurant terrace.

As Tom Lee laid out his theory, he would let loose with a laugh that seemed to well up from a distant mountain range, scree emerging out of solid stone that would pour down a slope, lasting only a few seconds, just long enough to make that sound of rolling rock, pebbles in a riverbed, mineral landscape, that's what evenings with Tom were like, feverish, convenient theories, and the breathy descending scale of his laugh.

5

DONOVAN CAN SOMETIMES STILL hear Tom Lee's laugh out on the patio of his ranch in Gold Hill, Colorado, a laugh that's not so much a laugh as a long, drawn-out sigh, expelled breath, thick and noisy but almost without tonality, almost nothing vocal about it, nearly everything contained in the breathing, a kind of exhaled laughter, propelled like a dart through a transparent blowpipe made from the hollow stem of a Bic pen.

Every time Donovan visits Tom Lee, they go out to the paddock to see the horse, all by itself out there, and growing thinner by the month. They lean their elbows on the fence, staring at the animal's contours, and Robert (that's the horse's name) makes no effort to interact with them, doesn't saunter over or even turn his head in their direction. He's standing in perfect profile, hardly moving a muscle, except for that occasional twitch that signifies he's on the lookout, keeping a sly eye on the two figures caught in his lateral vision.

And then they look up and out toward the mountains, the monotint in shades of brown, the peaks in the far distance, often cloaked in haze, creating a soft transition with the sky.

It's the place where Tom often comes at some point during his day to think things over, when he's alone, and this is something Donovan can sense, standing there next to him against the fencing, all those mumbled thoughts still hanging in the air from previous times.

He stares at the paddock, a bit of sky floating in the drinking trough, and he believes he feels the presence of those gnarled thoughts hung out to dry, the ones Tom never really believed in, that bear the marks of that disbelief, a little stunted, a little scrawny, pale-looking thoughts, bloodless, the waning troop to which Tom comes every day to add a few more sickly siblings.

The horse must also feel their presence, as he chews on a couple blades of dry grass he pulled up with his teeth, out of sheer idleness (he gets no real pleasure out of it), tasteless stuff, having lost all its chlorophyll, just grass-like enough to allow him to strike the normal pose of the horse grazing in its paddock.

At the risk of overstating it, you see a kind of resemblance setting in between Robert and Tom Lee, long-and-lean Tom and the rawboned animal, each more undemonstrative than the other, with interior monologues that must sound basically alike.

The last time Donovan was there, it had rained, turning the ground into a soft, slippery, ocher clay where their boots would get stuck. Tom Lee, hands in jeans pockets, wasn't saying much, so that you could hear very distinctly the sucking sound their boots made in the yellowish mud.

After standing there like that for a while, meditating the less than uplifting silhouette of Robert, they did their usual walk-around of the corral, a kind of long tracking shot as they moved slowly forward, with the occasional bumpy section, always leaving the fence in the foreground and the mountains in back, whatever the angle.

They'd necessarily have to stop every so often, to point something out, to remark on something material (what makes the fence so shaky in places, for example, how it'll have to be redone soon, the scaly skin of the fence posts that could use a new coat of paint, the level of water in the trough, and what to do about it, or not), or some aesthetic consideration—who knew?—sparked by the raw profile of the mountains (whatever you might think of them) that, even though they block the horizon, do so with such poise, or even some pop psychology comment inspired by Robert's bony figure, spoken ironically or in jest.

The tour complete, they walked back to the ranch, on that day when it had rained, squelching through the amber-colored mire. Their steps produced the same squishy sound, slow and complex, as each foot extracted itself from the muck.

This sound began to occupy a considerable place, it was a sound that brought them together, they the duo who were creating it, two rhythmic lines almost in synch, sometimes exactly so. They kept silent as they walked, their eyes on the sticky, clayey ground in front of them.

Apart from that, they'd spend the rest of their time on the patio, under the awning. During the day, the sun beat down hard, but where they were sitting, a kind of thermal truce had been signed. Shade is such a welcoming place, it defines a little island of well-being, not a bad place at all to spend some time.

On the low oak table, which must have been moved around a thousand times, as witnessed by the nicks and gashes in the wood (oh, my friends, the stories this table could tell!) that occasional wax and staining jobs have done little to conceal, Tom would spread out everything they needed: glasses, a bottle of bourbon, some cheddar cheese he'd cut into cubes with his pocket knife and served in a little dish which, no doubt, has some good stories to tell too.

On the previous visit, after cocktail hour, Tom Lee grilled some corn on the cob, which they then nibbled, eyes turned lazily out onto the prairie. Imagine the scene. Not a whole lot of notions flash into the mind at times like this, only the idea of corn, the idea of prairie, which aren't exactly jostling for elbow room in such an empty space as this, where they can so peacefully coexist; and also, no doubt, the idea of the other's presence, so close, all focused on his ear of corn, just like you, his thoughts fully occupied by the same things as yours: the corn, the prairie, and the presence of a friend, all three indolently overlaid in your mind.

And later still, the sun had gone down and they admired the crumpled colors that the sky had produced, the pink streaks, the ripped orange, all the stripes and slow discolorations, all very gradual and pleasing to the eye.

You'd have to admit that there are some spectacular sunsets on view from Tom Lee's ranch, and sometimes they'd stay out there under the awning, each one in his wicker chair, watching the way the night overtakes the day. They get all caught up in it, on days when the show is especially colorful, when it basks you in ocher and amaranth, coming at you with big broad brushstrokes, laying the majesty on thick, and how about a dash of Tyrian purple, and splat, here's a squirt of lilac.

Sometimes, they just took the girls back to campus, after the restaurant. Those dense nights compressed all shapes into unrecognizable entities. Only the buildings lit from within could resist, their facades forming random checkerboards that you could contemplate from out on the quad, where thick dark shadows flooded the lawns.

They'd walk a little, arms at their sides, or hands in pockets, or whatever, and then stop near a tree, for example, and say something, anything really, what mattered was that they moved in synchrony, a tender hand gesture, taking the other's hand in yours, drawing her body close, like that, with a little traction of the arm, and, as you finished the sentence you'd started earlier (timing is everything here), bring your lips to the other's face to snatch the kiss to which you'd been aspiring for a while now, the kiss meant to seal her deep understanding of *wabi-sabi*, and open onto a world of indulgence where just about anything goes.

The grass was drowned in the sticky tar of night (Oklahoma nights were like oil spills, flooding the landscape). The faux-medieval forms of the university buildings seemed to have dissolved, leaving only a bit of glowing stone here or there when a passing headlight would shine an accidental beam and momentarily illuminate some architectural feature with a splash of light, then quickly retreat.

And in the photon fizz of headlights, lips brushed, cautious at first, then engaged in sweet exploration, and it was nice to be standing, campus night owls trembling with desire, (yes, those grassy quads, I know all about them, too).

6

Donovan's car drives by new housing developments, clusters of units facing off across the street from each other, manufacturing community, but he's mostly driving through flat, undefined fields.

Trees grow scarcer, just the bare minimum really, mostly shrubs, anything that would introduce a bit of verticality here and there into all that horizontality, the infinite plain, where fences provide the only feature that lifts the gaze.

Fences, as far as the eye can see, running along the road, all painted white (a few red ones on occasion). Cattle herded inside, and metallic shelters for the horses.

And forming perfect right angles with the flat ground, slim telephone poles support multi-layer staves of electrical wire (it happens that blackbirds and their cousins will flock to some, placing their inky black semi-quavers).

Cornfields freshly harvested, short, decapitated stalks, dense and dismembered, as if they'd already grown too tall for this country, when they should have kept their heads down, where no one would notice, but no, and they have all been chopped down to the lumpy ground at the base of each stalk.

Donovan parks in front of the plate-glass window of a cafeteria that reflects the placid sky and, for a fleeting moment, the silhouette of our man, who locks the car and shoves the keyless remote into his pocket (press a button and lock all the vehicle's doors remotely, listening for that sharp click that confirms the vehicle's docile obedience—ah, the ephemeral, harmlessly pleasing sensation of power, the cheap thrill produced by the little sound of locks locking). Then, if you readjust your eyes, behind the glass's surface reflection (a bit like the fragments of an earlier poster that appear beneath the torn-away strips of the one plastered over it), some visual clues as to what's inside begin to appear: the red leatherette booths converging toward the long counter where the cakes of the day wait beneath their Pyrex cloche.

Donovan puts an end to these slippery optical tricks by entering through the glass door, not without first greeting the waitress, who, standing out front to get some air, is already wearing the defeated face of one who has landed completely by chance in a body too big and too heavy for her, the mound of flesh that seems like a randomly chosen receptacle into which she has been inserted by some awful mistake.

She follows him, ever destabilized by the size of the fortress behind whose ramparts she is enclosed (her tiny soul wanders the vast corridors of her colossal body, where she feels totally lost).

Once inside the cafeteria, Donovan takes a seat.

The guy sitting in the next booth is waiting. He's trying to absorb himself in the contents of a laminated menu in front of him, pictures of hamburgers capped by sesame-sprinkled buns set next to some French fries that look like a pile of pick-up sticks, pictures no doubt intended to get your salivary glands working, but which don't seem to be having that effect on the man. He looks around for something else in the cafeteria to focus on (any old thing would do, a potted plant to meditate, the conversation between a couple of customers he'd use as human specimens to study, imagining how they spend their days, how each one goes about life), but it's clear that something's gnawing at him. He isn't really concentrating on the role of the man who's come in to relax and grab a bite. How to fill the minutes that separate him, he hopes, from the arrival of the other, when that very arrival seems tinged with uncertainty (while he sits there doing nothing, blissfully ignorant of what's going on). His imagination begins churning out a few unlikely disaster scenarios that even he can't take seriously, but which darken his gaze.

When the front door finally swings open, it grabs his attention, and Donovan's too, but to varying degrees of intensity: the first man has a clear stake in it, his vigilance drawn immediately to the plate-glass door through which he sincerely hopes that a certain someone will enter; Donovan, on the other hand, raises a limp, incurious eye, more out of reflex than interest, however much we might all benefit from something new imprinting itself on our retina. But what's that I see, and that limp incuriosity gets surprised beyond all expectation, holy moly, how long has it been, Donovan wonders, as he makes a sincere effort to recall the last time, but comes up with nothing, anyway, it's been ages since he's last seen her, and he has no trouble recognizing her (one need only set to work those areas of the brain associated with facial recognition—occipital, fusiform gyrus, etc.—and link them up with your name recollection engine, located in some other region of the brain), and his heart leaps at this unhoped-for and joyous coincidence: Jane!

She moves uncomfortably toward him, and you can tell she's wondering whether he's waiting for someone else, whose place in the booth she's reluctant to take, imagining already the awkward mix-up that would ensue, the series of misunderstandings that would be difficult to undo, that she would not be witty enough to lightheartedly dismiss, as naturally as possible, the only way out of such situations, making everything utterly transparent and above board. But if it happened that he wasn't waiting for anybody else (Don't worry, Jane, reply Donovan's eyes, I ain't waitin' for nobody), the fact that he's alone at his table still doesn't authorize her to sit down and join him, since there's also the chance that he's alone because he actually wants to be, and she doesn't want to spoil his solitude by sitting herself down right there opposite him, smack in the middle of in his visual field, with her clumsy body stuffed into the red leatherette booth, stealing from him a moment that he'd hoped to have all to himself. One of those moments, and she understood him perfectly, necessary in everyone's life, where having coffee at some Formica table allows a person to get grounded and regroup, all those things she'd be loath to interrupt. And everything about her face delivers this apology for her perhaps unwanted presence opposite him at the table (because she's already seated by now), for she is the one who's suffering the most from this inappropriate gesture on her part.

There's always something uncertain about Jane's face, as if she were unsure she was the right person, always on the verge of acknowledging that this had all been a huge mistake, and that you had every right to point this out, if by chance you'd been thinking the same thing.

But this time everything is intensified by the situation, crystalizing into the pathetic smile she returns. It's very hard to react to that smile. Donovan feels incompetent and oafish, and sees that his gaucheness is only making Jane's impression worse. When Jane gets that look, you have to take her face in your hands and look her straight in the eye and say Jane, Jane, Jane, and kiss her face, applying your lips softly, don't press too hard, on her cheeks, her forehead, her eyelids, and keep calling her by her name, Jane, Jane, and that should wipe away the uncertainty, gradually erase it from her face. But as long as nothing actually authorizes him to do so, Donovan is finding it impossible to imagine any way to dispel it.

Jane folds her coat and sets it on the bench beside her, on top of Donovan's (it doesn't look like she's come to meet the man at the neighboring table, unless she's not showing her hand yet), and now the fabrics of the coat and jacket, tossed casually one atop the other, are making unchaperoned contact, random areas of each garment are touching, a pocket is pressing into a shoulder pad, a collar is brushing against a buttonhole, a pleat rests tenderly on an arm, and I'm sure that's not even the half of it.

So they carry on their little outerwear affair, taking full advantage of the owners' distraction.

You might even say, and I'm asking you the question here, that their spontaneous hookup provides the tentative game plan being drawn up in the cortex of the wearers of the garments, at least in Donovan's, as he stares into Jane's eyes with forced geniality, while all manner of dubious ideas are taking shape in his mind, setting off that old familiar inner struggle between warring parties which, although battle-hardened at this point in his life, are struggling nonetheless: let's do roll call, Desire? present, Shyness? here, and of course, Pride, your eternal ball and chain, Fear of Rejection, here I am, over here, while the more mysterious Fear of Succeeding is dragging its feet, but signs in present nevertheless, shooting you nasty looks. Things have gotten off to a bad start.

But the good news is that, at the other table, the late arrival has finally made it, in a sweat, all flustered and apologetic. He's the kind of person who has trouble relating to time and space in any precise way, resulting in much confusion. Still, he has the best of intentions, as witnessed by his gasping breath. But there is always something missing in his calculation, in the chain of cause and effect, so that even when he was giving it his all (you can see that he's gone to extraordinary lengths, a good faith effort by any measure), he already knew, with discouraging certainty, that his attempt at punctuality was in vain. Red-faced and perspiring, then, he sits across from his friend, distressed that he'd made him wait so long, he who always arrives at the appointed time, whether rain, or sleet, or snow, with the precision of a television news anchor.

The waitress brings Donovan his hamburger, and turns her same plaintive gaze to Jane, as if apologizing, once again, for the unsightly appearance which, as we now know, is not at all her own (What'll you have, sweetheart?), and Jane orders just coffee. The waitress takes the order and leaves, bumping into tables, and you'd swear she was steering from somewhere inside that ungainly body that she seems to be driving for the first time.

Donovan and Jane strike up a conversation, since there's no other way to go about it, if you're trying to gaze into someone's eyes without seeming rude.

You pretend to be searching her eyes for the progression of ideas that your words should be engendering, but in the meantime, you're admiring the amber glitter of her dark irises, and dead center, Jane's pupil aimed straight at yours, which means she's also looking at you as pointedly as you are at her (a frightening notion, no?), this way she has of looking right into your soul, through the black hole of your pupils, exploring the depths of your personhood. Into the craters of Donovan's pupils, yes, Jane has inserted tiny flexible probes into his most secret galleries, and they tickle on the way.

Look at him, the trembling, consenting, devastatingly happy target. And how is it that this look, at the very moment it makes you feel like you're dissolving, is the very thing that's keeping you in one piece? You're about to be pounded into dust, and yet she's holding together the very thing she's atomizing. You're riddled with holes, yet stitched together, undermined yet fortified, and the word bliss is starting to swirl in your head.

At the next table, they're chatting away.

They obviously haven't seen each other for quite some time, and the punctual one, who clearly has a leg up on the other, is still fresh and clearheaded, begins the questioning as one does (Family? Work? Love life?), and the other feels he's being bombarded as each volley drops. Still reddening, still perspiring, his hair a mess, a quarrelsome disposition, you get the impression, something tightly coiled inside, something itching for a fight. You can imagine a hologram of himself right there in front of him, his feisty, small-minded double waving his arms around, imaginary fisticuffs.

Motivated by far less complicated emotions, living out their sweet, mute lives as they wish, there on the bench, left unsupervised to play their tickly snuggly games, Jane's coat and Donovan's jacket continue to pleasantly anticipate their owners' embrace, which they're nowhere near as yet, Jeez Louise, sitting there so cautiously with a table between them, their miserable hands wandering its surface, trying to pick up signals, all antennae up, seeking and avoiding at the same time, with the distinct feeling they're in dangerous territory, attempting a forward drive that is noticed but not encouraged, though not discouraged either, withdrawing (even seeking refuge around the facial area of the person belonging to the hands, scratching the outside of a nostril that didn't even itch, rearranging a strand of hair that looked just fine as it was), then making fresh forays across the table in pathetically touching circumvolutions.

Donovan listens to whatever the river of Jane's voice carries along in its flow, details that are now far afield from the simple events recounted in her original story, muddying the stream so badly that it's now impossible to sort it all out.

He feels like the riverbed over which this river is flowing, Jane's words running over him so hard and fast that they're eroding his surface, carrying away parts of him in the rushing stream of talk, and leaving behind a fine alluvial deposit of what she had been transporting thus far.

He sits motionless, in thrall to the transformational operation he's undergoing, wondering whether Jane is aware of what's happening, if she can tell how the flow of her voice is washing over him, exfoliating him, while depositing a fine layer of mud, of clayey silt, Oh Jane, what are you doing to me?

Here's your coffee, hon (the brave waitress, so encumbered by her unwieldy disguise, as if her boss, for instance, had made her wear an inflatable uniform, inside which her actual tiny body, stifling in this impractical outfit she's wearing for the first time, is trying to make the best of it).

The guy at the next table continues to allow his hologram self to act out his pre-consciousness, this fiercely determined evil twin, filling the air with boxing maneuvers, jabs and cuts, while the man across the table holds up a punching bag firmly in his palms, allowing the blows to sink into the leather sausage, absorbing each one with an almost imperceptible start.

Let's share a piece of carrot cake, Donovan suggests, and a short while later, a russet sponge cake intercut with episodes of icing arrives, and they each plunge a spoon into their side of the dessert, digging a cautious path into this jointly claimed territory, careful not to take more than the other, no, they must stay within their assigned sectors, as they move ever closer to the median; and now, one has scooped a bit from a place where the other has just dug his spoon, proving that this differed mixing of saliva bothers neither, on the contrary, it's a first step, a signal sent to the other, who is free to receive or ignore it, but who in this case is receiving it loud and clear, and they focus their full attention on this ballet of the spoons that are carrying on their own private conversation right under their noses.

The storefront's wall of glass encloses them in the same protective space, like a transparent membrane allowing a clear view outside.

Chin in palm, Jane and Donovan are now looking at the outdoors, the light surfing over material surfaces, the sandy scenery, the parking perimeter sparsely dotted with trees, the slots where vehicles of various makes and models line up side by side, like some kind of automobile show, among which we recognize our protagonist's station wagon, ready for service (comfy suspension, automatic transmission, cruise control, air-conditioning, radio controls on the steering wheel, power windows, and as we've had occasion to observe, a remote lock system), and waiting for him, unflinching as the sun glints off the gray metallic body, and bits of sky get distorted in the windshield's curved glass, but who's complaining.

Out there on the other side of the plate-glass window, there's a different world where each of them is going to have to return.

They stay seated a while longer, thinking they could already be out there, somewhere under the trees, feeling the soft breeze brush by. Here, inside the cafeteria, the saturated red of the booths and yellow of the Formica tables, the smell of coffee and cooking oil, the tick of the percolator; out there, everything else, free and unpredictable.

They're going to have to go out there, immerse their bodies in the three-dimensional reality of the tree-shaded parking lot that's growing more insistent, putting increasing pressure on them, as if "what awaits them," as they say, is really waiting for them, tapping its foot with the tyrannical impatience inherent in delay.

They put their coat and jacket back on, and in doing so, tear apart the garments' furtive embrace, and it's too bad, isn't it, this coat and this jacket that had cuddled so adorably are now forced back into their erstwhile solitude (though the fabrics may well have conserved the fragrance of the other, who knows?).

Why is it that, when two people have feelings for each other, we want to see them embrace? It might happen, but the time's not right for that yet, and for the moment (they did manage to exchange phone numbers, which is already something), they bid each other a see-you-soon and shake hands, avoiding eye contact; then they walk out to their separate cars, without turning around.

Donovan closes the driver side door, aware of exactly how much muscular effort that act requires. He sits there doing nothing for a moment, easing himself back into the station wagon's cramped but familiar volume, before starting the engine.

Ready? Buckle up, pedal to the metal, remember you're supposed to get to the ranch by sundown.

7

THE ROAD IS A groove through the countryside that stretches out forever in two identical halves (pale prairie, as far as the eye can see) that rush toward the horizon, seemingly unrelated to one another.

It's one of those surprising phenomena that you may have already noticed, when the sky covering a single place can look like two completely different pictures, depending on whether you look to the left or to the right.

You look one way, and you see a luminous blue expanse, almost transparent, grazed by a few white scratches; look the other way, and you get a compact mass of gathering clouds that look like thick smoke rising out of a fold in the horizon. You could believe something was on fire back there, belching great puffs, sulfurous fumes, vapor of chlorides and oxides spewing from some volcano whose unsettled scores and suppressed anger have surfaced with a vengeance.

You seem to be driving right down the crack in the middle of this collage, the fissure separating the two images that might have bonded together.

There's just no possible continuity between these two skies, or even the two kinds of light they're projecting onto the prairie, the one on the right almost sparkling, while on the left, the light is flat and lusterless. The road is the caesura, and somehow or other, you plow your vehicle down the fragile frontier it has drawn.

This between-ness doesn't last. The cloudy half wins out, and it starts to rain, a drizzle so fine that the wipers only paint sludgy streaks of insect innards across the windshield without ever really wiping the glass clean, leaving a new yellowish trail with every pass, since the scarce water succeeds only in rehydrating and augmenting the dead matter.

Really, it's just a couple of unconvincing droplets that splatter the windshield and muddy the view, a stingy rain if there ever was one, and there's nothing to be done about it, since the wipers are now smearing instead of cleaning. It's discouraging, but without the wipers, this sprinkle would be distorting the view anyway, so it's really a no-win situation: the wipers, set at the lowest speed, an off-beat rhythm that's hard to anticipate, continue to do their damage, their piecemeal smudge job that's all but obscuring visibility, which only makes you curse your own forgetfulness when you realize that the washer fluid tank is empty.

When the rain starts falling harder, you switch the wipers to full speed, and they heroically repel the watery onslaught with renewed vigor. The mechanical movement tackles each new burst, tossing it to one side or the other, but the rain keeps coming, undaunted, slapping the windshield all the harder, erasing the outside world. These two unmatched warring factions pursue their unrelenting hostilities as Donovan looks on, his attention absorbed by the back-and-forth, the spectacle of their sparring match taking place inches from his nose, as his vehicle continues its push down the rectilinear, rain-spattered road.

There's something hypnotic about the beat of the wipers, and after several minutes of it, an old memory starts to resurface.

A few years back, for an entire weekend, Donovan walked around the little town where Jane said she lived, without making any special effort to see her; rather, he just breathed the air, telling himself that this was the air she was breathing, and that was enough for him. He walked for a long time, propelled by that contentment, not to increase the chances of running into her, but because, by simply walking around her town, he experienced a real exaltation, a driving force. At one point, he sat down on a bench along a pedestrian path and gazed at the somewhat neglected flowerbeds that edged the walkway. And there, as his eyes followed the labyrinthine meanderings of the leaves, or stared into the whorl of a corolla, moving from one plant to the next, lost in a tangle of stems or surfing over a crest of petals whose wavy extremities fluttered gently in the light breeze, he was thinking that all this profuse vegetation must have, at one moment or another, given the strategic location of this walking path, a place of recreation where everyone gathers when they want to be outdoors, attracted Jane's eye to its leafy convolutions, and this thought stirred him to joy, gave him the feeling that he'd stolen from her something she didn't know she'd given him, a covert meeting of eyes without her knowledge, without her gaze containing any question, probe, or judgment (in the unlikely event that she would ever judge him), but with a delicious impunity, committing this little misdemeanor unbeknownst to any of the unsuspecting passersby who thought nothing of this individual sitting on a bench, even though he was a stranger to the town, looking at the flowerbeds, which were there for just that purpose, after all, so that people would look at them and have an aesthetic experience, which is why he was able to let his gaze sweep over them, without anyone objecting, and drink in the same spectacle, the secret, mysterious, sealed vision, that Jane's gaze had encountered (maybe yesterday, or as recently as this morning).

And what was palpable and fragrant about the air, what everyone inhaled and exhaled without the first thought, was the same oxygen she breathed, in that same town; the breeze that grazed her nostrils (or her mouth, which sucked in great gulps of air), was the same one he breathed, so that her breath and his—hallelujah—were joined.

These memories flash through Donovan's mind amid a flurry of other ideas, carried along in his stream of consciousness, image upon image forming and vanishing, the way thoughts do.

The rain has let up a little, but the sky has brightened, rain and sun at the same time, streaming out of the sky onto the landscape (my grandfather used to say: look, the devil's beating his wife and marrying off his daughter). Raindrops sparkle in the sunlight, big fat ones, like a shower of glass beads; Donovan lowers his side window to let in the rain-washed air, the dazzling light.

So, there was this one time, I'm pretty sure Jane was there, a few years after they'd all graduated, when an alumni party was convened, and Keith showed up with a beard.

That month, no one knows exactly why, there had been a veritable epidemic of beards, and several of their classmates, their chins perfectly hairless the last time they saw one another on the campus quad, were now all rigged out in some ragged-looking facial growth that gave the overall impression of a bandana thrown over the mouth, or a scarf hastily drawn up over the nose (to protect against tear gas, for instance), in other words, something absolutely shapeless, something temporary and makeshift, there to provide a short-term service.

You'd have thought the evening's theme was masks, and that everybody had thrown something together at the last minute before coming, since the costume shop would already have been closed by the time they got out of work, for those among them who had "entered the workforce" (huge scare quotes, hooked index and middle finger of each hand raised on either side of the head); or by the time they managed to get out of bed, for the night owls among them, who hoped to enhance their creative powers by spending their inverted waking hours bingeing at bars and dance clubs, setting themselves apart from the diurnal masses.

Still, Keith's beard was a little neater than the others, not as bushy, which may have been the reason for its tidy appearance.

You never really know why some people grow a beard. Overall, it seems to coincide with periods of one's life that aren't the happiest. As if you were unwittingly displaying your little Robinson Crusoe complex, where the world around you is about as welcoming as a desert island, and that you're cobbling together a life willy-nilly. Your beard is characteristic of a rugged man who has landed in the middle of nowhere, and you feel it signifies all the personal ingenuity you're about to deploy in these less than ideal conditions.

There's an old saying, that a man who wears a beard has something to hide. These unkempt beards that seemed to sprout suddenly like weeds on the faces they now conceal most certainly signify something or other.

Keith, underneath his rather sparse beard, preserved his delicate air, which would suggest that his little trove of secrets probably amounted to no more than those of any average individual.

He recalled old stories of their campus years, and then, after a few drinks, he plopped down in a chair near a picture window, and against the luminous backdrop of the city by night, he withdrew into a reverie where you could tell he was brooding over some earlier ambition that he'd since had to scale back.

The fuchsia velvet armchair contrasted pleasantly with the cityscape view out the window, the twinkling lights against a navy blue sky, and Keith's slumped posture lent to the scene a placid, melancholic grace.

It happened to be one of those low-key parties where you could afford the luxury of soliloquizing on the passage of time, even though the revolution it had accomplished has yet to fledge, its traces left largely in the realm of the imagination.

You know the kind, those reunions where you get together after not seeing each other for a while, and in the first few moments, you think you notice differences, but they're only details that help update everyone's biodata, anecdotal elements that supply content for your conversation starters, and which turn out to be not so different in the end, and then you're all hey buddy, and it's the same old personality as before, you're glad to conclude, that essential something deep inside that emanates from within, unchangeable. It comes out in gestures and facial expressions, exudes from every pore, it shows in the way they move their mouths when they talk, the way they swallow their words or spit them out, the way they steer their sentences through the wet membranes of the oral cavity, because it's a very intimate thing, words coming out of the mouth. Finally, the nature of each person's presence, the individual qualities that radiate into a room, something you enjoyed back in the day, and which you can once again access, for the duration of this brief gathering.

Keith, and Keith's ideas, his opinions, which may well have shifted a little but were still recognizably his, those Keithian opinions, you could pick them out of a crowd. And Mike (you've already come across Mike, at the football stadium), and Jane, inaccessible as ever, and each of the others, all the same as they ever were, all convinced they had changed. And the little ballet of it all, early into the party, while people could still think straight, they'd saunter around, wineglass in hand, as if they'd decided to utter a single, very long sentence as they moved from one end of the room to the other, distributing a few words to each person as they went.

Later, amid the noisy confusion, came the inevitable

moment of self-doubt, a questioning of one's life that results from the contact with others, the cumulative effect of everyone else's news, their updated CVs, so to speak, since that's how people usually go about it when they've been out of touch for a while, mentioning a few concrete details with regard to job, marital status, your basic opening gambit at this sort of get-together. All that information, plus however many ounces of alcohol, would inevitably induce this moment—it was almost a chemical effect—a diffuse sense of failure that you were dragging from one room to the next, in the soft indirect lighting of the living room to the less flattering fluorescent-lit kitchen, where a small group would always gather, despite the overhead glare, preferring to make their solemn pronouncements against the background of sipping and chewing rather than infernal din of amplified dance music. And what they were all musing upon, from one room to another, was the disproportion between the grand designs they had imagined (remember, on the bench in the moonlight?) and the way things had actually turned out. The game wasn't over yet, big life changes were still likely to come, and one could still look forward to some mid-life achievements. But there is something about college reunions that tends more to ratify one's feelings of inadequacy than to revive waylaid plans, and here, there was a whiff of longing in the air that grew stronger as the party progressed, as if everyone were a carrier of freeze-dried wistfulness which, in the presence of all that alcohol, rehydrated and filled their glasses with fully reconstituted nostalgia.

And the longer the party went on, the more these ideas merged—the passage of time, the changeability of some things, the permanence of others, and the issue of where you fit in all that—swirling among the partygoers, stirring up a lot of stuff inside you, freewheeling, and you simply let it rumble within while you mingled, sticking to conversational generalities, since you were finding it increasingly difficult to focus on anything specific. The party was becoming a blur of color and shape, a complex interplay of body heat and room volume, something magnetic and abstract through the thick of which you had to steer your physical self.

The large front window revealed the first glimmer of dawn, watering down the midnight blue to something more pastel, the anthracite of a moonless sky yielding to softer gradations of navy, a pleasing backdrop to the red velvet sofa where Keith was presently holding forth.

The last of the guests were sprawled on couches and armchairs, or right on the carpet, paying varying degrees of attention to what Keith was saying, as he was the only one left in any kind of shape to construct anything approaching a logical argument. Donovan sat cross-legged facing Keith, he could see the curving outline of his silhouette against the deep purple, and through the window behind him, the city that was slowly emerging in the photographic bath of daylight.

Keith's face at that moment, moderately bearded, looking a bit rumpled against the red couch as he lectured in the dawn's early light, was probably the most recent image that Donovan could picture in his mind's eye.

And then there was Jason at the same party. You remember Jason, Donovan asked Tom, the last time he saw him, and yes, Tom Lee seemed to remember, yeah sure, I remember him, he mumbled, looking out to the mountains.

Jason would wander around campus with that peculiar walk of his, part sway part lurch, moving through the world in an uneconomical lateral swinging motion, like the intermediary stage of a mutant animal not yet fully adapted to its new milieu. He also had a way of shifting his jaw back and forth, supposedly to make sure he was chewing his gum on both sides of his mouth, but it made him look like he was mumbling all the time, while calling attention to the labrum that characterized his evolving species, awaiting further developments.

Clasped between his arm and his side ribs was a cloth-covered notebook where he would write poems as he sat alone under a tree, keeping watch from the corner of his eye, looking as if he feared someone might be about to steal it.

But none of them had any particular interest in Jason's poems, which were nothing but the tight little ball of pride he carted around with him everywhere he went, he the quintessential misfit, fierce and uninviting, striking poses intended less for others than for himself, postures that corresponded to the interior chatter of his little narrative about himself. Jason, no thanks, Donovan and Tom didn't really feel like hanging out with him, so he remained that stubborn silhouette, out of place and in love with himself, pacing up and down the walkways, an ambivalent poster boy for the maladjusted.

They did go with him one night to an open mic evening, where anyone who wanted to come read their work could do so, the microphone is open, which is the whole point. One person is scheduled to read, then anyone else present can sign up, and people take turns getting up to read. It usually happens in bookstores, but also in galleries, or anywhere that can provide a space for this rare, resistant speech that, for them, is what poetry means.

Jason took them to one of these open mic sessions in a gallery showing an exhibit of Native American art, run by a woman who claimed to be half Native American, since that's what people around here do, talk in percentages of Indian blood, when they're introduced to one another: How do you do, I'm half, how much are you?

Jason droned through two or three poems, blushing deeply the whole time, and then Chayton (one hundred percent native for sure) stepped up for his turn to read.

Chayton had a way of entering a room like a living reproach, his tensed body's sole purpose to recall the inglorious past of the nation's founding: a tightening of the abdominal muscles, the odd angle of his sternum, and the fierceness of his gaze, matching his overall look (his long hair, the silver buckle of his tooled leather belt, the way he wore his jeans, his "It's All Gravy in the Navy" sweatshirt), it was all of a piece, and you couldn't help but think, when you looked at him, that this was a survivor.

It was hard not to conclude that only some amazing twists of fate had made it possible for this man to be standing here today, he whose ancestors must have escaped the massacres, and thanks to their tenacity, had managed to produce this body, this person who eyed all the descendants of the murderers with unresolved rage in his heart.

And you would see him in the street, walking with that air of a tribal chief, and in his wake, the painful, legendary history of his people, whose narrative he would aggressively pound into the ground with each step he took.

So much for Chayton and Jason then. But I forgot one detail about Mike, and I swear this is true (you can't make this stuff up, as they say): he used to walk around campus with a pair of his girlfriend's panties in his pocket, and every so often, he'd take them out, have a sniff, as if he needed the morale boost, then stuff them back in his pocket and continue whatever it was he'd been doing, for example, talking with his friends who, the first time they saw him do this, started laughing hysterically, though they eventually got used to it, and considered it as natural as if he'd just popped a valium or whatnot.

8

IN THE END, DURING those campus years, Tom Lee became involved in writing a novel, and you'd see him sometimes, seized by some fresh inspiration, driven by a sudden impulse, rushing back to his dorm room, as if something were about to happen in his storyline and he had to be there to see it, to be present at just the right moment to discover the new plot element. He'd walk as fast as he could beneath the canopy of trees (or he'd hop on his bike, swaying as he pedaled, his torso thrust forward, his head positioned skyward to harvest ideas out of the clear blue gouache air); already, he was spinning some new threads to be woven into the narrative that he would have to hurry and write down, so that they wouldn't vanish, but also so that these fresh ideas would inspire a raft of even newer ones that he was yet to conceive.

Hours would fly by, and he'd feel spent, heavy and haggard, like after a long hike (muscles aching as he sipped some steaming java), and as he stared at the paragraphs that had taken shape on his screen, new bytes added to old, he was left with the feeling that, just maybe, he had actually produced something.

The working title of the novel underway was *Time Is of the Essence.*

You know the expression, a hackneyed phrase meaning that you shouldn't drag your feet, a useful maxim in any bureaucracy where the sooner you gather all the necessary paperwork, the better for your file. By way of example, the English Department secretary, Samantha, all one hundred and sixty pounds of her, located mostly in her chest and rump, invariably wearing a Lycra blouse that opened onto a nylon camisole thing she'd unearthed God knows where, made frequent use of it when she lectured the deadline-challenged faculty and students who never seemed to have the right paperwork, as she sat at her desk, behind her a bulletin board covered in thumbtacked pictures printed out in color onto 8½ x 11 paper, pixelated beyond recognition, mostly of her biological relatives, it would appear, including a nephew who played water polo, pictured smiling into the camera in his new swim trunks.

Of course, however secular the expression might be, it left one feeling vaguely meditative, pondering the twists and turns of time.

Tom Lee was undoubtedly too young at the time to have had much experience with time's meanders, for his subject matter ran out of steam and he never managed to finish the book.

Not to be defeated, he soon undertook a new writing project, a novel that would have been entitled *Nothing to Write Home About*.

It told the story of a guy who left home for no particular reason, no grievances or plans in mind, without really understanding how he got to that point, drifting around the big USA, first wandering around the state where he lived, then crossing over into another, and still another, making his way through four or five states. He walked or hitched rides, but either way, the landscape changed so gradually that nothing really took him by surprise. The prairie takes hundreds and hundreds of miles to turn into something else, same with the desert, and he felt like a Ulysses who'd have nothing to talk about once he got back home.

Since he started living at the ranch, Tom Lee has been working on yet another novel, again entitled *Time Is of the*

Essence, but based this time on a totally different premise.

That's about all Donovan knows, because once Tom Lee is involved in a book project, he feels the need to keep it to himself, so as not to stunt his desire to write by bringing it too much into focus. It has to remain a little fuzzy in his mind, and the fuzziness is what makes him want to write, to engage in the process of discovery. He embarks on a writing project the way you hack your way through a dense forest whose cartography becomes more apparent as you move forward.

Tom Lee sometimes says he could write another novel entitled *Nothing to Write Home About*, but which would tell a different story from the first (a man vegetating on a ranch somewhere, a thousand miles from anything, wondering why the fuck he left the city to bury himself way out here).

More generally speaking, Tom Lee is of the opinion that all books ever written could be entitled either *Time Is of the Essence* or *Nothing to Write Home About*, since these are the two themes that structure mental space: the issue of time, of course, and the fable of the prodigal son which has always haunted him, in all its many variants, including the prodigal father and husband in the figure of Ulysses.

Samantha's nephew, prodigal or otherwise, wrote poems about water polo, and every so often would send her one, in an email attachment, which she would click open on her screen and show Donovan or Tom, or any other Lit student that happened by, proud and a little wary, eager to show that there are some literary branches on the family tree, but anxious about what they might think of his talent.

And there he was, still smiling in the picture behind her desk, in his brand new polo uniform whose colors the printer had managed to bleed together, so that it was a little like he was standing there (a ghostly aura that the crappy print-out had produced) as you delivered your verdict.

At present, as he drives along the shady Oklahoma roads, Donovan wonders whatever happened to Samantha's nephew, whether he still has his swimsuit rolled up in the corner of some drawer, unable to part with it because of all the memories it evokes, or rather, all the promise it once represented, false hopes, in the end, but which were such a joy to behold back then. And where is that chest of drawers, what kind of house, if the nephew is married with a family of his own, and if Samantha goes to visit them on Christmas in their little clapboard home to have some turkey and shower her nephew's children with gifts she'd have chosen carefully for each, the way she does everything in her life, affectionately, anxiously, and in the end ineffectually.

How do you explain that Samantha never got married, a much-debated question in the dining hall, though back then, other people's lives interested them far less than their own, which were still so tenuous that they really had to focus.

Still, they returned consistently to the subject of Samantha, go figure, and to her Lycra blouses whose stretch fabric was strained to breaking point, laboring to enclose such heaving forms.

She'd been there long enough by now to have got together with some motherless, cougar-loving student, or a widowed professor with a taste for triple-D cups, or anyone else who may have been attracted by her pseudonym on a dating website (with its brief biodata that may have mentioned her nephew who plays water polo and writes poetry) and who was truly hoping to settle down and start a family, so that, at present, he's the one she's having breakfast with, feasting on pancakes in her bathrobe before going out to do some gardening.

9

YOU HAVE TO WONDER, when Donovan isn't there and those lonely days start piling up, and Tom Lee goes down to check the water level in the horse trough, whether he ever starts talking to Robert, even just a few sentences. He claims he doesn't, but it's easy enough to imagine him there, leaning on the fence, right in front of the anxious animal that has not quite come to terms with the fragile barrier that separates him from the rest of the world (the gleam in his eye, the way the muscles beneath his coat twitch incessantly, something fearful and impatient in his hooves, ready to bolt), falling naturally into a one-sided conversation, intermittent utterances broken up by breathy silence that keep Robert on the alert, still immobile, ears pricked to capture sound waves.

One can only imagine the secrets Tom Lee has poured into those ears, secrets that Donovan will never hear, that Robert will never tell, which might explain the horse's unengaged attitude when Donovan comes up to the fence whenever he visits, his slight look of equine contempt, a blank stare that gives nothing away, Tom Lee's phlegmatic confidant, psychologically removed from the present moment, a bit like a therapist who refrains from saying anything and lets his own mind wander, far from his patient's, into the meanders of his own life.

That's Robert, playing the non-interventionist shrink to Tom Lee's need to talk, while carrying on his own horsey monologue that has nothing to do with Tom Lee's more articulate speech, but which is just as sensitive to the present situation, the way the paddock is set up, the sandy ground, the rectangular shape of the water trough (where little bits of sky float on its surface, vibrating slightly if there's wind), the limitations imposed by the fence, the unregulated flow of speech that this proximate individual is aiming straight at him, whose sound waves strike his auditory apparatus without making the least bit of sense.

That old thing? No way, I swear, says Tom Lee, claiming he'd rather talk to the kitchen sink than to that big hunk of horse meat grazing unconvincingly a few feet away, old Robert who just vegetates in his paddock and couldn't give a hoot about Tom (which I have to think is probably not quite true).

Anyway, it's not very healthy for animals to be talked at, Tom thinks, and he's got a theory to prove it, as he's often explained to Donovan. The three or four words, let's say, that their brains can retain, okay fine, but all that chatter, all the logically constructed arguments and incomprehensible soul-searching projected into their eardrums, and which translates into nothing but noise, no, he's not in favor.

So, if you have to talk, talking to inanimate objects seems much saner, more honest and direct, less devious, less complicated with regard to what we expect in return, since, unlike animals, objects offer no hope of any kind of reaction.

Even giving an animal a name, said Tom Lee (I never call the horse Robert, only when I'm thinking about it to myself, when I say to myself, Hey, I'd better go down and check Robert's water level, or maybe in conversation, you and me, we'll say Robert, right? but with him, I respect his anonymity, it's the least I can do), there's something dubious about that. It's obviously convenient, in all sorts of circumstances, but if you ask me, it ends up giving him a sense of his individuality—there, I said it, the "i" word—and makes him aware of his physical place in the world as an entity subsumed under a proper name. And it's amazing how easily they adapt to it, Tom Lee went on, dogs and cats, I mean, while in their own lives among themselves, barking or mewing to each other, I'm willing to bet that no personal names ever cross their animal lips.

And along those same lines, I don't know whether you've ever noticed, but there are domestic animals, pets, I mean, that have lived so long in the company of humans, looking them in the eyes, responding to the name they've been assigned, obeying commands in a way that signifies not only their docility, but especially their capacity to understand, that they end up, since they have no other point of comparison, believing they're human too.

It's a fairly common phenomenon. Just recently, I was looking out on the beach at Trouville from my hotel window, and there was a dog, off leash, walking along with a group of four men, clearly believing it was an English gentleman among equals, never falling behind or getting ahead, looking calmly to the left and right with an air of one who's enjoying the view and the company, never displaying any kind of dog behavior, like sprinting ahead then rushing back, or playing tag with the waves, digging joyfully in the sand or running circles around its masters, no, it simply conformed to the pace the men had set, walking their walk, if not talking their talk.

I think you could argue that personality disorders like these would not emerge if animals were left to huddle in their namelessness.

Without names, Tom Lee rationalized, the notion of personality would never occur to them; they would simply go about their business as daily necessity required, without wondering who they are, sheltered from the vast masquerade of likeness and imitation, without risking the kind of alienation that results from hanging out with the clothed species whose interests do not necessarily match their own, and assenting to engage in their modes of communication.

Tom Lee concluded that it was an act of violence against nature to speak to animals, whereas if you talk to your coffee pot or a lump of sugar, unlikely but not impossible, at least you won't be upsetting their mode of existence.

So, if you asked him, Tom added as a coda, to each his own, the horse, the coffee pot, and himself, each one taking full advantage of the harmonious and specific potential that such a life involved.

Robert, for one, seemed to be out there grazing, in utter ignorance of his name.

And not only that, but there was no way of knowing how Robert felt about things, apart from what one might construe as a vague dissatisfaction (food wasn't great, no mares around to seduce) and a tendency to turn inward, yes, an introverted animal, by all accounts, whose internal monologues were unavailable to the outside.

Because there are animals that look like they're talking to themselves.

I'm not familiar enough with horses, but dogs are a good example. You look at them, and not only do you sense that they're thinking about something, but you have the distinct impression they're getting those thoughts across. You pass in front of them, and see them staring at something that isn't there, something they want to happen, but hasn't yet, the crinkled skin above their eyes, as if they were furrowing their brow under the weight of the thoughts they're having. It's no mystery, what they're thinking about, you could produce an accurate transcript every time, you know exactly what they're mulling over, what they're waiting for, what movie they're making in their little minds; because when they're waiting for something, there's a whole scenario in the making.

They're keeping watch, for instance, for their master's return, tied up in front of some shop, or from inside a locked car (or

sprawled on their doggie cushion at home), and you can be
sure that they do entertain the possibility that the master will
never return. The notion gnaws at them, and becomes the main
thread of their monologue, the specter of abandonment that
pops into the mind, dancing its little dance, that's just the way
dogs are, nothing you can do about it.

Or another case (and this could be a cat or a dog), they position
themselves in front of a hole in a wall into which they're pretty
sure they saw something small and mobile disappear, and stare
at it intensely, head cocked, you know the way they do, that
funny twist of the neck, that wicked look that means they're
about to pull a fast one. Of course, they're waiting for the little
varmint to come out (why else stand guard?), anticipating how
fast they'll have to act, all focused and on the alert, a one-dog (or
cat) rapid reaction force. But at the same time, look closely and
you'll see the shadow of a doubt taking shape, despite all their
concentration and vigilance, a deeper questioning as to why
they're waiting there in front of the hole in the wall—it's been
several minutes now. Is this really what they wanted, had they
chosen to be there of their own free will, is this how they really
wished to spend their time? Had they really had any choice
in the matter, or were they driven by that die-hard ancestral
instinct to lie in wait for hours at a time until something,
anything (usually a mouse, but most often, they didn't even
have the time to ID the thing, a silverfish, some tiny insect,
nothing worth the trouble, really) reappears. And as they wait
for something to emerge from the gap in the wall, they ponder
that irksome question that produces those wrinkled foreheads
I mentioned earlier, the ones you'd swear were knitted brows.
It's very easy to imagine the dilemma they face, when part of
them wants to stay there in front of the baseboard and wait
for the damn critter to reappear so they can pounce on it, but
another part is thinking of the pattern in the carpet in front

of the warm fireplace, of the soft cushion where they sleep, of the doggy bowl still a third full, or that old plastic bone the master brought home one day, out of the goodness of his heart, and presented with great fanfare, where did that thing get to anyway, it must be around here somewhere, and that they can gnaw and scratch a little, making believe it's fresh kill.

But with Robert, it's very different. Whatever is going through Robert's head will always remain a mystery. He looks at you with an impenetrable blankness that's sometimes hard to take on days when you're feeling all by your lonesome. Go ahead, just try and figure him out, and then feel the force of his contempt, how utterly indifferent he is to whether or not you can divine his thoughts. It's not that he hasn't noticed you're there, no, the shuddering of his body shows that he's detected you in his field of vision, but you're just not someone worth interacting with, that's the impression he gives. It'd take one clever bastard to know what's going on behind that muzzle, those jaws, that forelock.

10

THERE WAS ALSO THE summer of Buridan's Ass.

You know, the philosophical paradox in the form of a fable, where an ass, or donkey if you prefer, having eaten or drunk nothing for days, is feeling equally the pangs of hunger and thirst, but prevaricates when presented with a tub of water and a sack of oats. His endless dithering—should I start with the oats or the water, let's look at the question rationally, he says, and proceeds to methodically weigh the advantages of starting with one or the other, but the two options come out practically even where these pros and cons are concerned—further weakens him, and he dies then and there, having touched neither grain nor drink.

It would appear, then, that having two equally desirable goods within one's reach can prove a paralyzing liability if you're incapable of choosing which one to pick first. The exercise of free will is compelling in principle, but, let's face it, tricky in practice.

Here's what went on that summer.

Two satellites were orbiting around planet Tom Lee: a certain Amy McGibson, who was sending him fairly explicit signals (or so it seemed—such matters always depend on the interpreter's competence) as to her level of interest. And a certain Maggie Chambers, whose feelings for him were less obvious, though a few searing glances may have been interpreted as encouraging.

Let's look at the forces at work.

Amy McGibson was a tall, lanky girl with aquamarine eyes who sported an air of elegant disenchantment wherever she went. She was rumored to have broken many a heart, with an effortless seductiveness resulting from the simple mathematical addition of height plus aquamarine eyes plus disenchantment.

Maggie Chambers, conversely, was on the small side, and a little chubby, let's admit it. But on the plus side, she had lively eyes that changed from a whole range of greens to beige and brown, and on rare occasions, to blue. And Tom Lee just loved to dive into them, to feast on their ever-changing color show, never the same twice. No lie (he said, drawing lovingly on his cigarette, his expression gentle, sitting there on the back of the bench, looking lazily into the moonglow), it was a beautiful thing, like those toy kaleidoscopes he used to stare into for hours at a time, so long ago.

Okay. So here was Tom Lee's problem.

His attraction to Amy and Maggie was not—and he pondered his words carefully as he delivered them to Donovan and Keith—of a strictly physical nature (nor was it that physical-chummy type either, where there's no commitment apart from listening to the other's doubts and fears during pauses in lovemaking, and trying your best to somehow respond, to propose an appropriate solution, the pithy, one-sentence feel-good piece of advice, sure anyone can do that). Both women, Tom thought, had the potential to become someone whom, you might say, he could spend some serious time with.

Since Tom had never felt that way about anyone, he wasn't at all prepared, and it didn't help that he was getting hit on by two girls at once. Amy and Maggie's temperament and physicality were so at odds, what you could guess about how they saw the world through those long lashes was so different from one to the other, that if he were to choose one girl over the second, he would also be opting for a lifestyle entirely distinct from the other girl's. He wouldn't have the same take on things, and he would soon find himself undergoing small changes to his own being, but a different set of changes from the ones he'd undergo if he were with the other girl (he knew himself well enough that he would never be able to resist this kind of transformation). So he had to think twice before getting too involved with either.

And this is how Tom Lee ended up spending hours and hours daydreaming on the campus green, in pretty much the same state as that moronic donkey that couldn't decide between oats and water.

Whenever Keith Hassanbay would toss in his two cents' worth regarding love and relationships, he'd paint a pretty discouraging picture.

Here's what Keith Hassanbay had to say.

Hassanbay said that all you had to do was look around: people who lived as married couples felt stifled; and among bachelors, those who moved from one relationship to the next concluded—Vanitas, O Vanitas!—that earthly love was empty, while those who had no sex life at all withered away.

Maybe it was just a problem of redistribution, Keith hopefully hypothesized. Maybe the ones living together with someone would have been better off single, and the multi-tasking bachelors might have made perfectly happy spouses if they had ever tried to settle down with someone; as for those still languishing, they should have given more thought to which of the two categories they'd best belong to.

Maybe.

Then Keith would pluck a dandelion, plant the stem between his incisors, and twirl it like a weather vane, as if indicating the proper direction for them to take—though if you asked Donovan, he'd say the flower looked more like a Ferris wheel, which indicates nothing at all, just turns on itself in a movement of conspicuous leisure, getting no one anywhere.

Sometimes, Keith and Donovan would attempt to apply themselves to measuring the pros and cons of a relationship with Amy or Maggie, but they lacked conviction, and their theorizing would degenerate into idle talk, utterly inconsequential.

Tom Lee used to test how it would feel by talking about the person he was thinking about, as if, by merely pronouncing the name, uttering a few sentences about her, he was already making oral contact with her, as his words made their way through his throat, palate, tongue, and lips. So that, although neither Amy nor Maggie were yet orally familiar, literally, with Tom, their names, and all the words that had been used to describe them had emerge a thousand times from the caressing action of his mouth. And every time those names surfed briefly over his tongue and brushed against his lips on their way to becoming words, he experienced a thrill like none other.

Donovan's ears were not particularly sensitive to those names, but they picked up what Tom Lee was saying with the somewhat bookish fervor of one who knows that friendship is based, among other things, on such phenomena.

Lying on their backs on the campus quad, their heads like keystones of a vaulted arch, their arms extended, eyes riveted to the sky as they contemplated the slow progress of cumulus clouds, sheep safely grazing in a blue meadow.

In the end, late that summer, Tom Lee wrote each of them a long letter, taking the greatest care in each case to fasten upon the special way he felt toward her, the particular feelings she aroused in him. He tried hard to get beyond the framework of comparison and enter into each one's uniqueness, to steep himself in the fragile, subtle, and irreplaceable elements that each one had to offer. He took great pains to tell each what he understood of her, why he had sought to reach out to the scintillatingly wonderful person that she was.

In other words, two letters that had nothing to do with each other, each written in sharp focus upon its subject, and which—you don't even need to ask—he never mailed.

And didn't he have every reason in the world not to? The most obvious being that the simultaneous arrival of the letters in the girls' mailboxes would trigger a cascade of unpleasant situations for all concerned, while sending them one at a time, waiting for a reaction before sending the other, would require choosing who would be first, and the act of choosing, as we know, had been our hero's stumbling block all along.

All of that notwithstanding, as a general rule, it's not so smart—look me straight in the eyes—to send love letters in the mail. Everyone will eventually write one at some point, that seems inescapable, but getting them to their intended receiver, I don't recommend it. Such baring of the soul might prove embarrassing later on. Or she could make fun of you, or find it creepy, in any case, it could ruin a perfectly fine friendship, a less emotional one but pleasant nonetheless. And most especially, think of the risk of finding yourself embroiled in the consequences of sentences that, while they expressed exactly what you were feeling at the time of writing, might well have lost some of their truth value in the interim, and in the harsh light of day.

For all these reasons, Tom Lee didn't send the letters, but they did inspire a novel he entitled *The Summer of Buridan's Donkey*, which, while depicting both young women, made manifest the clash of feelings experienced by the young male protagonist, dramatizing the choreography of campus life as focalized through one person's uncertainties and desires, some of which translated into those first, scary, timid experiences, while others never made it out of the gate; and then those second ones, fast-moving and unpredictable. In other words, two antithetical sensations that you feel while looking down upon the vast masked ball of college life from your lofty perch: novelty (the impulse of discovery) and déjà vu (the uncanny illusion that, paradoxically, only youth can produce, that you've seen it all before).

It amounted to a rather long-winded dissertation on the possibility of multiple objects of affection, polyamory, if you will, and on the triad of desire, love, and friendship, his conclusion being that the three could accommodate diversity quite nicely. Desire, well, that one's obvious; and friendship is the baseline, although there may be a few bad apples that let jealousy get in the way; but what about love? Ditto. Not only measured along a timeline, where, hallelujah, we can picture loving several people in succession, contrary to what the old pulp romances tell us. Or better still, among those we love one after the other, we continue to love the earlier ones (isn't that reassuring, in a way?), in a kind of sedimentation of the heart where each love leaves a layer, consolidated and indestructible. Not only that, but at a single point along that timeline, two people (or more, why not, four or five), and exactly as it happens in friendships, equally sincere, in other words, though nourished from different sources. The personalities of each object of affection call up a different range of emotions, but which all come under the general heading of love. Love adapts each time to what we think we perceive in the other, to the context in which your coming together takes place, to what you expect, give, and receive within that context, and to the thousand other details, mostly unspoken, just as would happen in friendship, where we sincerely like a person, totally and differently from every other friendship we've made.

And that's what the young narrator discovered, lying on his back beneath the changeable American skies.

The summer of Buridan's donkey came and went, without Tom Lee ever tasting the lips of Amy McGibson or Maggie Chambers. But the novel, picked up immediately by a literary agent, sold very well at the bookstores, and many readers were certainly able to relate to the slacker protagonist, and the way he screwed up both relationships, since he was never able to commit to either.

The pathetic side to this failure (all the more pathetic in that that it took place in summer, when, as we all know, falling in love is much simpler, bodies come together with less resistance, with fewer material complications, the warm air making our initiatives flow more easily) struck a chord, because Tom Lee's readers, for all their swagger, have had their egos bruised by the ways of the world. And in the secret of their private reading, they felt reassured to find a fellow loser in the novel's protagonist. They felt sorry for him, in a way, though a nascent sense of superiority emerged from this initial sympathy. Yes, superiority, since, all things considered, they were managing pretty well, they would say to themselves, perking up all of a sudden—novels are good for something, aren't they?

It should be said that in the novel, the main character, named Sam for the purposes of the fictional plot, ended up thinking it wasn't only Amy (renamed May) and Maggie (now called Jo) that he had to write letters to, but all sorts of other girls to whom he felt the need to open up, to express the exact nature of his feelings toward each of them, to dissect their relationship in order to identify what was unclear and what was specific about his attraction, what form each attraction took in his mind, and how a possible relationship with them might unfold, while at the same time analyzing the points of resistance that might explain why they weren't getting anywhere yet, and the steps that might be taken if either party should want to move things forward. With all this in mind, he wrote seven or eight heartfelt letters, which he never sent, whose function was not to seduce the girls, but to help him get his bearings, to define, if only temporarily, the position he might occupy in the turbulent astrophysics of his life, where a young man has to locate his central axis and balance the rotation of his own personal planet.

I'm not sure Amy and Maggie recognized themselves in Tom Lee's book. By the time it came out, Maggie had disappeared from the scene, and no one ever found out whether she read *The Summer of Buridan's Donkey*; as for Amy, she had a word with him about her reading one time when she ran into Tom Lee in the dark hall of some campus building where, protected by the relative obscurity of a dimly lit corner, she complimented him politely on his writing style, but went no further than that.

Tom, on the other hand, had thought so long and hard about both girls while writing the book that he came out completely exhausted, with the conviction (obviously deluded) that he had learned everything there was to know about them, and that it was time to move on.

11

FOLKS HAD TO FIND something to do with their evenings in the little town closest to the ranch where Tom Lee had landed one winter's day, braving the snow drifts that accumulated here and there, finally stopping and getting out of his station wagon to put on the tire chains, not a simple operation when you're by yourself. By the end, he'd be puffing great clouds of steamy breath that slowly lost their compactness against the white and brown backdrop of mountains. Other stories had begun to emerge out of the hours the locals spent at the town watering hole, taking shape inexplicably, as if they got them from somewhere else.

These stories initially had to do with the reason that had brought Tom Lee to the ranch in the first place, since these folks would occasionally drive by the house and see Tom Lee sitting under the overhang or leaning unenthusiastically against the paddock fence. At nightfall, when they all got together, they seemed to agree that this cowboy exile must have had something to do— they were vague on the details—with a botched love affair with a woman named Linda, who haunted his lonely nights.

However they managed to get wind of the name, Linda—Lin, to her friends—did really exist. Donovan had caught a glimpse of her one day when he went to pick him up at the apartment Tom shared with her back then, and he could probably have given enough details for a facial composite if asked, with all the uncertainty that such an exercise entails.

The locals don't have the first idea, which doesn't stop them from launching undaunted into a detailed physical description whose theoretical exactness floats just above the foam on their beer before dissolving into the next subject of conversation.

What's certain, the way they see it, is that she had a "special kind of beauty," (or maybe it was "her own kind of beauty," yes, that was it, and "her own kind" was not meant euphemistically here to salvage some quirky facial feature that violates the consensual canons, endowing it with that tricky but usually positive notion of "one's own"; no, it was intended for emphasis, an accent on the quality that said Linda could not possibly be confused with anyone else, a certainty that they'd broken the mold when they made Linda, something that precluded the prospect of someone else stepping in, like it or not, none of those substitutions that one accepts as a rational alternative but ends up actually liking, you'll see, she's not so different), a beauty that instilled in this abandoned man's heart the poison of irreplaceability.

A regrettable feature for your live-in lover to have when she packs her bags and walks out on you, one autumn evening, leaving you alone with the prospect of a long winter ahead.

Something that could explain why a man might leave his apartment one day, an apartment where he had spent the last few late-season weeks stewing, never leaving the confines of his living space where dirty laundry, empty beer cans, and all manner of refuse were creating a garbage rampart, a fortress around his fragile heart, get into his car and, defying the elements, drive all the way to this ranch at the end of the world, inquire as to whether someone might want to rent it to him, and in the end, stay there for good.

On the subject of Linda Burn, Tom Lee has always been perfectly tight-lipped with Donovan, curled up around his secret, storing deep in his gut the compact, friable aggregate of his time with her—a fragile little meringue, like baked Alaska inside out.

Tom Lee fritters away most of his time on the front porch sprawled on a wicker chair, allowing the benefits of this intermediate space to work their magic, a space that's neither inside nor out, fully engaged in the landscape, yet protected by the porch roof, both in the world and in the house, and you never need to get out of your chair, the complete double experience of what it means to exist.

How many hours did Tom Lee spend staring out at the mountainsides, sitting under the porch roof, I don't know if I mentioned it before, with his old Remington typewriter right in front of him? He developed real feelings for those mountains. Gratitude, above all, for aren't they simply always there, faithful, grandiose, and benevolent? They raise their profiles like guardians, enormous vigilant bodies overseeing the prairie. They reward him with their presence, almost like muses, keeping careful watch over his work, gentle and proud, lofty and attentive.

But resentment too, before such an unflappable, immovable mass, the way they just sit there, annoyingly slow-witted. The very opaqueness of such a wall of rock brings the gaze to a halt, making it impossible to see beyond, preventing the prospect of an infinite perspective dissolving into the vanishing point. The garrote of mountains gagging the oppressed prairie, and you stand there with a sense of mounting fury. By the end of the evening, and with the help of a few shots of bourbon, wouldn't you say, you're hurling your choicest insults at them, here's lookin' at you, ****ers—and one could easily imagine, right around sundown, that some traveler who's lost his way and ends up driving past the ranch would spot the looming silhouette of Tom Lee, clasping a bottle, spitting his favorite profanities into the face of the mountain, something about mothers and sisters, and that seems to calm him down, once he's gotten everything out, with that twisted grin of his, everything he has to say to that damn mountain, holding nothing back, and he'd fall back into his wicker chair, drained and exhausted.

Truth told, our Tom Lee has been known to lose it every so often, all by himself out there on the ranch, with no one but Robert, just offstage, skinny old nag that he supposedly never talks to, and the mountain that stares back at him in silence. He exchanges a few poisonous glances with his Remington (nasty-looking contraption, its arms like raised tentacles, the characters at the end of each starting to look like evil eyes), delivers a few tenderly heartfelt smooches to the whiskey bottle with a loud smack in the fading light, or goes inside and harangues the sugar bowl, which also needs a good talking to every once in a while.

Because I haven't told you the story about the sugar bowl yet, have I?

Tom Lee had got into the habit of talking out loud inside the house, a sentence here, a sentence there, nothing formal, the kind of thing we all do, asking himself why the fuck he had just entered a room, for example, or some obligation he'd contracted and needed to keep repeating to himself as a reminder, the kind of conversation you regularly engage in with yourself to check off items from your list of chores, or to remind yourself of chores to come. But he also talks to objects, the ones he deals with on a daily basis.

So, you can see him in dialogue with his coffee pot, long face-time chats, with the pot looking best in profile (let's call it a she, shall we?). He tries to soften her up with compliments on her slender waist (you know which ones I'm talking about, those metal Italian two-part gadgets that twist together, water in the bottom, coffee grounds in the middle, with a curved black handle, doesn't she look terrific, like a stylized shock of hair), and tells her his dreams of the previous night, blurts out grand pronouncements that she listens to with rapt attention (but isn't she inserting just enough distance, just enough cool collectedness, for him to start thinking he's really interested in her?).

They spend every morning in each other's company, so you have to believe he has the right, if only to keep his vocal cords limber and to remember what it's like to talk with someone, to produce a narrative fragment or two for her, through which, over time, he gives her some insight into certain aspects of his personality.

But he doesn't neglect his less frequent companions either.

The sugar, for instance. He'll shout out for it from the other side of the room on days when he feels like taking the bitter edge off his coffee.

The sugar sits in its bowl, keeping to itself, trying to look small to escape notice, not realizing that the ruse makes it the most obvious victim. I'm sure this has happened to you: by acting like you don't get it, in an effort to deflect attention, you end up as the focal point despite yourself. At some gathering, a meeting, for instance, you don't want to be called on, so you slump low in your seat, scrunching your head between your shoulders, stare blankly at nothing in particular, try to look a little lost, while inside you're saying not me, please not me, with the result that, even though they hadn't thought of you at first, they seem able to hear the refrain of your unvoiced plea, as if your very reluctance allowed them special access to your thoughts, and they suddenly turn to you, Say, how about, and they pronounce your name, and say Why not, after all, and ask for your consent, but as far as they're concerned, it's a done deal, you clearly can't refuse at this point, your heart is pumping, you're sweating, your little pantomime was not only useless, but it led you to the very place you were trying so hard to avoid.

The sugar, as I was saying, sits in its bowl, keeping to itself, but Tom Lee is no fool. He walks over, grabs the sugar bowl, and extracts the recalcitrant cube, and before scalding it alive in his coffee, he holds it between his fingers and looks it over, chiding it a bit for trying to hide like that, no, that's not very nice, is it, trying to outsmart me, were you, thought you could get away with it, did you, what do you take me for, etc. Anyway, I didn't mean to bore you with all that, but it's a fact that Tom Lee entertains himself like this in the solitude of his ranch, just to make sure he still knows how to speak, and when need be, animates any number of the tons of inanimate objects in his immediate environment.

But it has to be said that his most intense relationship is with his Remington.

It's an old machine, I haven't told you this yet, that he found it on the ranch the first few days he was there, one afternoon when he was attempting to find a place for all the stuff that the owners had left lying around. In the chiaroscuro of one room, shutters partly open, allowing a shaft of strong sunlight to pour into the dim room revealing a jumble of mostly useless junk, a sweaty Tom Lee managed to extricate the old Rand model, a little grimy but still in working order, and a cardboard box containing rolls of typewriter ribbon, red and black, still in their plastic wrappers—totally alien objects in today's world, but which I used to use at one time (guess I'm from the olden days, I tell myself), sitting at tables where, amidst the clatter of keys, I typed out my first stories (I've kept a roll, still in its wrapper, on a shelf in my study, and it looks for all the world like some archaeological specimen whose function is long forgotten).

It was a Remington exactly like the ones you see in photos of American writers from the fifties, and Tom Lee, having dug it out of the pile, he thought, or rather, he said to the machine, You, my friend, meaning that it wasn't going back on the heap where he'd found it, that the two of them had a future together.

Starting today, we're in a long-term relationship, you and me, it won't always be a bed of roses, just so you know, I'm a seat-of-the-pants type of guy, with a bad case of self-doubt when it comes to relationships, as if every moment spent with someone else were liable to be the last. He would experience this same undermining insecurity with the Remington, and it would pay the price, but at least they would live out their chaotic story together under the porch roof, enjoying the sharp contrast of shadow and light, looking out on the blank, dun-colored page of mountains forever staring back at them.

The Remington put up no opposition. He dusted her off, spruced her up, and set her solemnly on a low table in front of him, sat down, leaning slightly forward, folding in two, a position that compressed his gut; he stared at her for a long while, elbows on thighs, fingers a steeple under his nose, indexes pressed against his mouth. And in that stare lurked the cohort of doubts that had plagued him forever, making their regular rounds, but also, uh-oh, here we go, also hope, since even the most skeptical temperaments continue to harbor a secret belief, fresh hope born of this new situation, for this special occasion, about to get put through the wringer, no doubt, but which did put on such a brave face, all bright and cheery, ready to measure itself against the private militia of doubt that continued to make the rounds, a certain bluster in their step, the self-assured swagger of the lawless, yes, here come the doubts, zipped into their suits, nightsticks clipped to their belts, which they would not hesitate to use, since that's what they were there for.

And use them they did, almost immediately; but until then there was still that honeymoon afternoon, and surges of rekindling, especially in the morning when he would sit across from her, still sleepy but happy in a diffused kind of way, for no other reason but the hope he placed in her. And which she would dash, of course.

Things soured during the day, mostly. First, he'd leave her there while he went and took a nap, wherever he felt like sleeping, on the couch, in bed, in a chair, it made no difference. Then, later that night, he'd start swearing at her, or giving her the stink eye.

Maybe she felt hurt, offended that he completely ignored her all afternoon, with that annoying, passive-aggressive attitude people get when they're mad at you but decide not to say anything, cloaked in their self-righteousness, only making matters worse, their resentment showing all the more blatantly, all the blame they refrain from laying at your feet, even though they feel they're in the right, playing the martyr. And he counters, saying he's not getting anywhere with her, You see, we're not getting a thing done, he says to her in moments when he's still able to keep his cool; nothing good can come of such an admission, which usually heralds the beginning of the end. Still, they stay together, one of those couples in crisis you hear so much about, a brittle pairing, yes, but at the same time, you have to wonder what powerful force binds them, how, despite repeated, corrosive admissions of dissatisfaction, they somehow stay intact, never allowing any crack in the edifice to bring the house down. Or is it just force of habit, their weariness at the prospect of change, their inability to draw the obvious conclusions, a reproach aimed at them by those haughty, nasty, types who can just pack up and slam the door behind them, because their survival depends on getting the hell out of there.

Which is exactly what Linda Burn did, throw her stuff in a suitcase and leave. Over in the next town, tongues wag endlessly about Tom Lee and the ranch, rehashing the Linda Burn story and the day she packed her bags and walked out of the apartment, walked down the street already strewn with the first fall leaves, setting out for who knows where.

12

You'd think they'd known Linda Burn all their lives, the way they talk about her, especially after they've had a few beers, and you have to wonder how they arrive at a consensus on all the details.

As sure as if they'd seen it with their own eyes, they'll describe the coat she had just enough time to throw over her shoulders, how it was liable to slip off as she stamped out of the apartment, strong-willed and miserable, and into the alley that separated her from the street and her newfound freedom that, once she had walked through that front gate, would represent the first step into the next phase of her life.

They could also call up the image of her cumbersome suitcase that she carried in her right hand, setting her off balance, her wobbly body forming an arc, leaning heavily to one side as a counterweight, both excited and ambivalent about her decision to leave. It took moxie, but left her drained. She felt a buzz, there was no denying it, alongside the inevitable pang of separation, even when you're the initiator of the split, it's heady and horrible all at once, and you know it as well as I do, that turning of the page.

When the gate of the residence clicked shut with that familiar metallic clang, it resounded this time as never before, as something definitive ringing in the air, and Tom Lee, who'd been leaning against a wall, slid slowly to the floor and sat, curled up in a ball, thinking that the sharp, violent sound he'd just heard came at him like someone spitting in the face of what, from now on, he'd have to call their past.

Linda Burn heard the same sharp metallic clang behind her, but it sounded to her like the bell at a boxing match, the end of a round. Saved by the bell.

She turned down the little street that the change of season had already begun to drain of color, and walked between the brick facades, her overweight suitcase straining her wrist, a boxer stepping out of the ring where she'd just boxed her final match, in breach of contract, unceremoniously returning home, a free agent now, alone and without a plan, unsure of what the coming days would bring.

The road continues to cleave the landscape, and you drive through what has become your medium, following the blacktopped strip that has come to define a left and a right. And also, yes, a front, where you're heading, and a back, where you've been, a receding undulation. The car is the measure of all things, organizing the space through which it moves.

Occasionally, the silhouette of an oil rig (Oh, a pump-jack, Donovan exclaims), whose characteristic nodding motion looks like the only living thing in view, in this land of sparse vegetation and lonely silos. It looks like performance art, an installation of dynamic sculpture that might signify the pendulum swing, the scansion of time, the urge to access the earth's remotest depths; the pump itself is a gigantic steel insect, a beast of prehistoric proportions, reminding you of visits to natural history museums where you stood at the foot of full-scale dinosaurs and looked up at their terrifying maw, imagining what they must have been like, running through the fern forest, a plant-eating species, the didactics inform you, to your great relief, and likewise, the enormous metallic pump grazes the prairie, backlit against the clear blue sky.

You drive by fenced-in stud farms and equestrian training grounds, russet cows, beef cattle and bulls, the occasional bison, look, there's a couple of them in that enclosure, alone with the fading memory of a wilder, ancient time, waiting to be turned into ground meat, apparently less fatty than beef (Have you ever had a buffalo burger?).

Even llamas, there's one right over there, and poof, it's gone, the time it takes to formulate the words, already behind us.

A wall of hay, rectangular bales stacked like bricks, whizzes by on the left, just a dot now in your rearview mirror.

It all just flies past, you barely catch a glimpse; it's when you're on a road trip, forgive me for stating the obvious, that space most resembles time.

Long trips are apt to make you rethink your life, as if the fleeting nature of the landscape streaming past your windshield almost inevitably makes the metaphor seep into your consciousness, like it or not.

Driving gives you license to daydream, something that comes with the territory (and couldn't be further from your couch potato self stretched out on the sofa, whose threadbare cushions and lumpy, uneven stuffing have seen better days), and instead of the two or three images that normally spring to mind when you're just lazing around the house, a long drive naturally catalyzes the process of self-examination and a reconsideration of your life path thus far.

Now, if you were to ask me about what ever happened to Amy McGibson and Maggie Chambers, I'd have to say, full disclosure, that two or three years ago, Tom Lee came across Amy McGibson and Keith Hassanbay, by total coincidence, in a street of a small Colorado town, where he saw them walking hand in hand.

He shadowed them for a while, not daring to approach, trying to guess, from the way they were walking together, how involved they were with each other. Amy's small hand enlaced in Keith's larger one, was this just a spontaneous, friendly gesture, a way to keep in step as they strolled? Or did it promise more, was it merely the first stage of a blossoming affair? Or worse, was this the easy-going manner of two people who'd already worked through the preliminaries? All sorts of scenarios flashed though his mind: maybe they were living together in this town, or were they just visiting? Was this their first little getaway together, or just another outing among many? Was it a spur-of-the-moment decision, or had they been planning this trip for months, gazing at the unfolded map on the kitchen table beneath the cone of light, tracing with their fingers the route they would take, deciding together on their itinerary? He was having trouble stemming the tide of all the questions rushing into his head as he fell into step behind Keith and Amy, mechanically obeying instructions that seemed to be coming from somewhere else.

Of course, the broader question had to do with where they were going, and not just for the next half hour (if he kept tracking them, he'd eventually find out their short-term destination), or for tonight (what little love nest in which hotel room, or which airport terminal where they would bid their sad farewells), but for the days, weeks, and months to come, it all goes by so fast.

The reader of Keith Hassanbay and Amy McGibson's love story abandoned it mid-chapter: Tom was left standing there on the sidewalk where he made the sudden decision to stop playing this little game for fear of being discovered, renouncing all hope of getting the full story from them (Hey Tom, hello! Really, you hadn't heard?), or picking up more clues the longer he tailed them. Instead, he watched their silhouettes move down the broad avenue, inevitably shrinking as they went, nothing to be done about that, while Tom's gaze, seeking an escape from all these disturbing thoughts, lifted toward the vertical panorama of the mountains which, at the vanishing point, rose up at the end of the street, edging the town on all sides, rolling and massive, taking up half the sky.

As for Maggie, she wasted no time marrying a guy she met at some campus party, a certain Bruce, originally from Livingstone, Montana, and the whole gang was invited, Tom, Keith, Donovan, and the others, a lovely Montana wedding, with all the canonical festivities one might expect at a traditional ceremony—but which also provided latitude for guests to wander, as all good weddings should, in search of some private encounter with another guest they might be meeting for the first time, those sidebar activities that make weddings so much fun. Some of which, you'll admit, aren't always in the best taste, especially when a tipsy guest with a candid camera captures a scene on video, however fuzzy and wobbly, where we hear Donovan and Tom, unmistakably inebriated, saying some pretty unflattering things about the groom.

Wasn't that the very least he could do when he'd spent an entire summer ogling the bride, even going so far as to fictionalize their love in a novel where, granted, she'd been weighed against another girl, but was still the model for one of the two female protagonists that had won the hero's heart, and who, at present, in her creamy wedding dress, was trading niceties with the groom's distant relatives she was meeting for the first time, amidst a noisy social swirl, enough to make you sick to your stomach.

More than the wedding itself, which did leave a few group scenes imprinted on his mind, all the fancy backdrop décor, the live swans, the extras in flashy colors that recomposed the tableau as they randomly moved around the landscaped party area, Donovan recalls the videos taken with night vision software where everyone came out grayish-white or blue, looking like the living dead.

Some were shot in front of the door to the restroom, where a small congregation of drunks had started gathering, each one holding forth with no regard for whoever else might be spouting off, as in some absurdist drama, entire sentences emerging three or four concomitantly, no one seeming particularly offended that their words were falling on deaf ears.

Others were filmed outdoors, in secluded areas of the garden where people were sitting on the lawn, smoking God knows what. The trees were black splotches in the Montana night, shadowing the pasty faces of the fringe crowd that had decided to go off on their own and smugly make fun of everything about the wedding and reception, the groom topping their list, of course, the name that just kept coming back, *I'm tellin' you guys*, the one nobody could ever stand. They dug back into their campus days, where everyone seemed able to provide a piece of evidence, dredging up old grudges and grievances they'd kept to themselves until now, dumping them in an inebriated hate fest in the cool night air, the vegetation coughing up its carbon like an old consumptive, and absorbing their words.

Donovan and Tom came upon Mike sitting under a tree (you remember Mike, right?). After dropping out of college, Mike's only plan was to hit the road, to drift around in search of no one was quite sure what. He wound up in a tiny mountain town, home to a former singer and a few groupies of some sect or other, just to mention the ones he could actually categorize, since most of the townsfolk were too plain to label, either as individuals or as a group. You'd find most of this motley crew at the town's only grocery, something straight out of a western, your typical General Store, and everything else was conifers and rocky outcroppings, with snowcapped peaks in the distance, white tablecloths draped over mountaintops.

Mike badmouthed the groom with the best of them, even scoring points for some particularly choice digs.

His date was a plump little blond, the uninhibited type who'd look you in the eye and smile, and there was something in Mike's voice that seemed to be saying, or somehow suggesting, that he'd be glad to share her whenever they liked, and that seemed to put everyone at ease. Okay, and here, I probably shouldn't be saying this, but she was acting like she wouldn't mind being shared, though you can imagine that she probably thought of her personal freedom in slightly different terms. Her platinum blond hair caught the light just right, and looked great in the night vision video setting, all silvery and overexposed, so that when she leaned over one guy or another, that was all you could see.

So they kept on like that, getting ever more inventive with their slamming of the groom, while the blond made the rounds, never dropping that smile of hers.

She was wearing a flowered blouse, very seventies, and a miniskirt of the same vintage, having neglected to include any undergarments.

The almost full moon shone above, taking stock of the scene, blindingly white against the black sky, raw, not a hint of haze.

In short, an ordinary wedding, with its façade of respectability, and your average shenanigans in the wings. And even the façade was showing some cracks, as happens when the groom, completely smashed and realizing that he wouldn't be in any shape to perform his nuptial duties, figures he might as well make a complete ass of himself and starts insulting his bride, his mother-in-law, and their guests, who decide to toss him in the pool to cool him down.

Out of which he emerged, staggering a bit but proud of himself, a forefinger pointed upward toward some unidentifiable object, probably whatever point he'd been trying to make when he got dunked, a sentence that seemed to be hovering free and silent just in front of him, instead of inside his head where it would begin its normal course through his vocal apparatus and into the world outside.

Held up by two friends, one under each armpit like a pair of human crutches, our groom attempted to walk, index finger still raised to that elusive, unspoken statement as it inched forward in the Montana night, and which he pursued, leaning on his two acolytes, struggling to make out the amorphous contours of its meaning, eyes and mouth wide open.

13

THE LANDSCAPE GRADUALLY CONCEDES to the notion of relief, a distant edging, only on the horizon at first, as a promise, a prospect only hinted at.

Then the horizon slowly asserts itself.

You see mountains rising out of the earth in waves, bluish in the distance, still easily swallowed up by the rows of trees rushing by your side window, cutting off your view. Even an average-sized hillock in the foreground can obliterate them.

These are the same mountains that one could imagine Tom Lee gazing at from the vantage of his ranch, sitting there in front of his Remington. They're wearing their ironic look today, when the air is perfectly transparent, sharpening the edge of the visible world. Nothing like their sullen cloudy-day scowl, an almost pensive, dreamy air that smooths their roughness. No, today's mountains are distinct, ridges etched against the sky, nobody's fool. There's nothing friendly about the way they look, no indulgence in their attitude. Their mute materiality leaves you completely alone, your flesh trembles before a rocky mass so ill-disposed to dialogue. Still, Tom will occasionally have a thought for the fauna which, although invisible at such a distance, must be roaming around up there, living within the great pleats and folds of the mountains, wending their way along its creases. The inert rocks are thus a reservoir for living things, filling him with a sense of solidarity for his fellow creatures, and the mere idea of it cheers him up a bit.

Let's imagine a little breeze this time. Just enough to lift a few light objects on the porch, to rustle the tablecloth or blow a crumpled sheet of paper a few inches across the floor, in fits and starts, like a stone skipping across the surface of a pond.

And Tom Lee stands there idly looking at the inanimate universe of his porch that the wind blithely sets in motion, asking no one's permission, a kind of high-energy puppeteer rushing around, trying to work in several places at once, flapping some cloth over here, stirring a bit of paper over there, a real mischief-maker who couldn't care less about what the owner might think, making a mess of things, marking the scene with a personal taste for polyphony. You hear the cloth beating against the table leg, the paper scraping against the surfaces as it rebounds, the stone moaning as it whips by: the wind is a one-man band imposing its chaotic racket, as if hoping to garner some small change. And Tom Lee, feeling a little light-headed, could easily dig into his pocket and find a quarter, that's good enough, which he'd toss to the wind, here you go, now beat it, go mess with someone else's stuff (and the wind would sheepishly pick up the coin, etc.).

Tom Lee, and maybe I forgot to mention this, wasn't making much headway on his novel, so in a flash of inspiration, he started in on a short story told from the point of view of the coffee table, a prosopopoeia of sorts, where the table tells the story of its life, how it was brought here in on a horse-drawn cart, how all the successive occupants of the ranch lived, their family histories, love affairs, and murders. His head is abuzz with ideas, all alone there on the porch, drunk as a skunk, typing away like mad on his Remington to bring to life the misadventures this table had witnessed, how often it had been mauled and manhandled, couples in heat sprawled atop it, meat cleavers whacking through sides of beef laid over it, all the vicissitudes to which a table might be exposed, out on a ranch in the middle of nowhere, all the way to when Tom Lee moved in and Donovan started his regular visits, their man-to-man conversations, and the short story comes to a close in the present of the writing act, where the table supports the Remington and Tom's glass of scotch and describes this most recent tenant, who's banging away on the keys, raising his eyes every so often to gaze out at the mountains.

If you look at the mountains long enough, you start to see shapes, as if a paid illustrator working for the "Games" page of a magazine had concealed some animal figures in a complicated background, for readers to seek out and identify.

Tom Lee and Donovan have been known to play the guessing game themselves, when they haul their wretched carcasses onto the porch in the morning, their faces looking like dough kneaded by sleep, pounded and puffy, sagging and shapeless. They stand there looking out at the mountain, scanning the zones of light and shade, the abstract figures forged by their overlap until, out of all this geometrical non-figuration, a sleeping lion's head suddenly pops into focus, the ineffectual guardian of the mountain whose color blends with that of his mane. And it's as if the rest of the mountain were nothing but an outgrowth of the lion's body, a congenital hump of some sort, unless it resulted from a brawl, and having gone untreated, developed into a monstrous deformity, the kind that hurts in wet weather, the onset of pain acting as a forecaster of the coming rain, in fact, when his whole body becomes a barometer, his aching bones announcing a rise in humidity.

Maybe that, or maybe the head of a lizard, slowly detaching from the whole, bald, a bit fuzzy-edged in its monochrome beige range, but its eyes are lively and alert this time, visibly open.

Or maybe a field mouse, or a lemming, the whole body, curled up in its light brown fur.

Or even a crocodile, and with a little luck, its mouth wide open, showing its long rows of teeth.

As the light changes, so does one's perception of the terrain, so that the mountain conceals a whole bestiary for us to uncover, an infinite variety of animals tucked into its rocky crags and crevices, whose camouflaged bodies we're free to hunt and reveal.

Which is exactly what they do in the pleasantly regressive fatigue of early morning.

Because morning fatigue has nothing to do with the nighttime variety.

Night fatigue yearns for sleep, its natural endpoint. It functions as a symptom, a red flag that warns you it's about time to call it a day and leave the waking world to go knit up the raveled sleeve. You can try to fight it, to hold your ground, to drag your feet in the face of repeated injunctions, but sleep will carry the day, in the end.

It will tear you away from the little pleasures of consciousness and steer you toward your bed. Even if you resist, your head will start to nod, your eyelids will drop in spite of themselves, while life all around you will continue in your absence.

This is why night fatigue is rarely pleasurable: it brings to a close, it cuts short, it removes you from a situation.

Morning fatigue, on the contrary, moves to dispel, forming a fleecy buffer, a transition to your fully operational use of the day.

It's indulgent, full of vague promises that we want to believe every time.

It was in this state, then, lumbering and numb, yet feeling equal to the task, that our two friends would squint toward the hidden bestiary.

Tom's room on campus looked out onto the quad, so Donovan would occasionally go there to work, since his own window came right up against the back of an athletic building, the one housing the swimming pool, completely blocking any view, especially when the giant exhaust fans would click on intermittently, sounding like a fiery dragon in its death throes.

He would shove Tom's Formica table against the windowsill and sit facing outdoors, drinking in the green as he waited for the next sentence to come.

Most of the time, Tom would be there too, lying on the bed reading, making all sorts of microscopic noises, how could he do otherwise, an itchy sweater, a turned page, an occasional sniffle or (the worst) the drumming of fingers, the underlying scansion of his interior monologue that revealed to anyone listening the rhythm of his train of thought. But Donovan considered these noises (which, if you started paying attention to them, assumed outrageous proportions) as a kind of incentive. The room was Tom's, after all (who didn't seem to mind having his furniture moved around), and however annoying Tom's presence might have been, it was also an inducement to work, a living body breathing the same air, infusing the room with the power of an indolent muse, a joyful force to be reckoned with.

Donovan allowed the masses of chlorophyll that seeped through the windowpane to massage his eyeballs and enhance the cortical functions of reverie and language. He tried to delicately extract from their hiding place a few well-turned sentences, which he would then read aloud to Tom—he owed him at least that much—as the price for occupying the best spot in the room.

He sometimes went and sat outside at one of the nice outdoor picnic tables provided by the campus, the ones with the bench firmly attached to the table, just in case it would cross your mind to walk away with one. He'd breathe in the moist, grassy air that rose from the lawn, and he felt one with nature, though these moments of exaltation were not always the most productive.

While Donovan vaguely surveys the landscape, his mind between two memories, wandering from one idea to the next without settling on anything in particular, I'm thinking back to Tom Lee's theory about animals and how risky it is to talk to them, to ask that they participate in an utterly perplexing world that isn't theirs, where they go about sniffing at the manufactured objects on their path, awkward and at a loss, finally sitting down in the middle of your carpet, proud despite their split personality, staring at you with that questioning look, that major, ongoing, anxiety-inducing question that continuously haunts their existence: what exactly is it that connects them to you, what are the similarities and differences that characterize their relationship with this clothed, talking being that feeds and pets them, berates them, and most importantly, includes them in their life? Since the only way to recover from all that exhausting self-scrutiny is to sleep, these animals spend the better part of their days and nights unconscious, as you've surely noticed, seeking refuge in dreams of a wilder life, their muscles twitching as they imagine themselves leaping through meadowlands (for it's only fresh air, the great outdoors, the thousand little creatures all about, the way they propel their bodies through the tall grasses, rub against the wind, it is these things alone that remind them of their true nature).

There is certainly truth in all that, but when you see how they look at you sometimes, be they lizards or birds or what have you, we might well wonder whether they aren't the ones who are trying to communicate with us, and not the other way around.

I say that with great caution, however, since I don't trust my judgment in this area, I'm well aware of my St. Francis of Assisi complex, the delicious inner turmoil I feel (sorry) when I look into the eyes of an animal, especially a wild animal.

This is between you and me, but when my eyes meet the

jaded gaze of a caged lion that stares wearily back at me the way it would at any other visitor to the zoo, I want the lion to be addressing that look to me, me specifically, and in the space of that gaze, to wordlessly communicate everything it can about the conditions of its incarceration, and its gratitude for the opportunity to open up to someone through this eloquent exchange of glances through the protective fencing.

And since I mentioned lizards, I take special delight in those moments when one of them appears on the warm flagstones of the terrace where I'm sitting, standing stock-still when it senses my proximity. And here is where our eyes meet, and I can almost see it processing the data, assessing the threat level posed by my presence, the same question asked at every encounter with another living creature. And there on the terrace of the house where I'm a temporary guest, I want it to understand that the beam of my gaze is a kindly one. I want this dumbfounded but decent little being to take an interest in finding out something about me, I who wish it no harm, as it will soon discover, I who am nothing but curious and attentive to its way of seeing things, of getting on in life. I want it to see me for who I am, to look directly at me, Christine, though it doesn't know my name, of course, and to know that I see it for what it is, as an individual lizard. And perhaps, later today when it's about to sleep, spontaneously reviewing all its day's highlights, it will recall our encounter (as will I, no doubt, as I snuggle under the covers in this house where I'm a guest, and remember the eye of the lizard), it will conjure up my silhouette, sitting on the flagstones, looking down at it.

14

THERE ARE SEVERAL VERSIONS of the Linda Burn story in circulation, but they all agree on three main points: the time of year when the breakup took place, the fact that it was Linda who left the apartment under the wavering descent of leaves (twirling as they fell, half-dead forms filling the air all around her), and also what they all called "her own kind of beauty," a blurry category whose details belong to the eye of the beholder.

The time the townsfolk like best is when they can take advantage of a newcomer who, like themselves, sits at the bar and orders a beer or two, since that's the only way to forget that the great wheel of time has brought night upon the land. They knock back a few, shoot the breeze with whoever is standing there doing the same. Mug after mug, they launch into increasingly meandering and open-ended discussions, as if on a water slide, landing on their butts with a big splash in the great pool of notions. Eventually, as always, they come back to Tom Lee's story, the guy living all by himself out on a ranch, not a single head of cattle, just an old nag that has to be on its last legs, believe me. Just two or three years ago, in the dead of winter, when no one with any sense would dump his sorry ass in such a place, this dude moves in, and here, they take turns giving the new guy at the bar all the details, Tom's city origins, how he's only been around for a little while, how hard it was to move there in the worst possible winter weather, the solitude of his daily existence, how he just sits there staring at the mountains;

well, you know, all the stuff you've already learned, what anyone who hangs around long enough is bound to find out.

But their favorite moment in the long exposition comes when they turn to the newcomer and look him straight in the eyes, a look that says that any city boy who shows up in the middle of winter in a place like that and seems in no hurry to leave must necessarily have something to hide.

What happens next is amazing: the newcomer's face, his eyes, all his facial features, even below skin level, make it very clear that he's suddenly imagining the most outrageous scenarios. In a matter of seconds, he has plotted several horror stories with the greatest of ease, rather stunning when you think about it.

That's what keeps the locals busy, when a stranger steps into the bar's artificial light, its dreary yellowish cast, but with the advantage that it doesn't seem threatened by diurnal shifts, maintaining a steady, dim glow even as the sun sinks into the horizon. Outdoors, the transition to night is always a little off-putting, when you realize the day is dying and there's nothing you can do about it but watch, helpless, until night comes and drapes the earth in its terrible shroud—and you escape out from under it to go bask in the bold, heroic electric lights of the local bar.

You want to know how Tom Lee and Linda Burn first met? The locals have a version available for you, and all you have to do is head over to the bar and they'll deliver it, you don't even have to ask. There's always at least one guy who'll come up to you and offer to serve as your narrator.

Tom Lee and Linda met at a gas station, it's as simple as that, one summer day when the ground seemed to shimmer beneath the gasoline vapors.

The bright logo, the glass booth where the attendant in his slate-gray overalls was working the cash register, it had to be over one hundred degrees outside, the air unbreathable, clothes sticking to your body, and in this unbearable heat, you felt the curious desire to rejoice.

One car, then a second, drivers enclosed in their solitude, a few words exchanged as they unscrewed the caps and began pumping, each one next to his, her vehicle, the amounts in gallons and dollars clicking by on the meter, and finally, an invitation to go have a sandwich in the frigid air-conditioned discomfort inside.

Now we're inside, day-lit interior, low hum of refrigeration, various neon signs snaking around the glass walls, secreting cool tints that contrasted with the sunny exterior, the open pages of sandy earth, and above, the monochrome blue stretching to infinity outside the plate glass. There, Tom Lee and Linda Burn bit into their sandwiches stuffed with ingredients they'd checked off a list, as is customary in these lands (standing there, side by side, leaning against the counter, pen in hand, wondering out loud what they should order, finding out about one another's tastes, how sweet, those getting-to-know-you moments, those careful, quivering early steps, happy as they trade their foodie confidences—hard to argue that this doesn't count for something); and between mouthfuls, they manage to slip out a sentence or two about where they've been and where they're headed.

Itineraries are meant to be modified, and the two cars ended up following each other, eventually stopping at a restaurant where they dined on hamburgers before getting a motel room, your average faded wallpaper décor, Formica closet, check, fake leather chair, okay, and here it comes, a king-size bed, upon whose fancy bedspread (a sea of brownish cotton in raised wavelets) Tom Lee laid Linda Burn down, and without removing her clothes, started talking to her, enveloping her with words (along with his warm hands) whose purpose at this point was unclear, whether they were meant to heighten her desire, or to compensate for the uncertainty of his own, or to weave a cocoon of sentences around her, strong enough to keep her prisoner for a time, the time Linda Burn would be spending with Tom Lee, quickly moving her stuff into his apartment, until the day came when it was over, when she threw her stuff back into the same big suitcase and slammed the gate behind her, as we've already said.

While they were at it, the good townsfolk felt no compunction at telling you all about which positions Tom Lee favored with Linda Burn, in the apartment he shared with her.

It was an apartment he'd been renting for quite some time, the one she came to live in with him almost as soon as they'd met, bringing along with her what you'd call her personal belongings. Like a newly adopted kitten, she was quick to learn how to carve out a little territory for herself, to establish her preferred routes, to select favorite places to curl up and read, or sprawl out, soft and supple, almost adhering to the shape of wherever it was she had landed.

The bedroom blinds were lowered against the glare of neon and street lamps (and when there was one, a remainder of moonlight that lazed over in the western sky like an old crust of bread left to dry out on a plastic tablecloth, but which managed to seep through the Venetians and bathe the room, barely diluting the nocturnal color), but the local gossips still seemed to have no trouble giving you a detailed depiction of the way he'd lift her off the mattress that was set right on the floor, where they were already locked one inside the other—here's the scene: he lifts her off the mattress (which is on the floor) where they're locked one inside the other, and without disengaging, he stands up, her legs wrapped around his waist, and they keep at it, in the middle of the room, with no support, just like she asked him to, the first night, when they talked about it in the dim light of the motel room where they started touching, slowly, full of desire yet reluctant, each in a separate world. Not on our first time, she whispered, when he questioned her on the subject, coating her in his words, stroking her hair, touching her still mostly clothed body, her voice trembling with all the future possibilities shimmering on the horizon, the first time should be simple and sweet (and since he asked, as his hands and mouth were getting a little ahead of the game, Tell me how you'd like it, if it's okay my asking, do you have a way you like it, there are guys who act like waitstaff in a restaurant or something, And what will the lady be having today? Hmm, I can't make up my mind, can I choose more than one?), but for the second time, and all those thereafter, they got into the habit of that one position, a reward of sorts, something he was more than happy to do for her; it's like a dance, where he penetrates her while carrying her in his arms, she's a perfect fit, his grip is secure, they do their back-and-forth right in the middle of the room, spinning and laughing. With equal tenderness, he lays her back on the bed after they've both come, and still coupled, entwined, they snuggle, catching their breath, as he strokes her hair now and then.

Truth told, Linda had seen Jack Nicholson do this move in a film where he was having sex with a somewhat chubby girl, and he held her exactly like that, standing up, spinning around the room, that's the way she remembered it anyhow, though she couldn't recall whether he was really dancing inside her (pretending to, I mean, for the purposes of the shot) in the middle of the room, or whether the camera was tracking around them, or whether he was standing on a revolving stage of some sort, but that was the effect, in any case. Which is why they called it the Jack Nicholson position, one of my favorites, she told Tom Lee, now that he had performed it so well for her.

Tom Lee had done a lot of rock climbing, and you could tell that the way he went about things sprang from those lessons learned, how to evaluate his anchor points, decide his best angle, feeling around her body as if it were a boulder, searching for the right grip, assessing a cantilever, a slope, thinking in terms of steepness, escarpment, levels, and dips. He's conscientious, efficient, and rational, which may come as a surprise to you.

Anyway, that's the way they describe him, standing there with their feet on the footrest under the bar, giving full rein to the imagination when they sense the moment is right to broach the subject.

Tom Lee, unlucky suitor, but a scrupulous guy who had made love to Linda Burn as best he could. But he had his inner world, and who knows what else, that had driven Linda to pack her bags and hit the road, some little grain of sand that had jammed the flawless machinery of their trysts, some sense of inadequacy, a reproach, a regret, or was it simply that urge to leave that can strike at any moment, in anyone's story.

And they go back to their beer mugs, soak their lips in the bitterness of a liquid whose lovely amber color beneath the foam seems to contain all the promise in the world.

And so, yes, when Tom Lee sits there like some inert rock, facing the mountains, his full weight pressing into the chair, aware of the gravitational pull on his body mass that is sinking vertically into the seat, while the rest of his volume organizes around this force, not a single thought crosses his mind; when he's there facing his mountain, with Robert outside the frame in his paddock, poor beast, chewing on solitude and dry grass, no longer able to identify which taste is which. But when he's sitting at his table across from his Remington, with its spindly tentacles waving ambiguously, and whose black plastic keys burned his fingertips this morning, it's a whole other story, a matter of stemming the fear, grabbing that fear by the ears like a little rabbit that will eventually wiggle itself free and scurry off into the background before disappearing in the straw-like grass.

The Remington, crouching and evil, flashing louche looks, tentacles raised, a single letter at the end of each, only one, minimal mono, so that you hardly know what to do with it, quite frankly, twenty-six of these singularities glaring back at you, it's unnerving, what do they expect you to do, and how to be sure you're giving them what they want. It's a contest now, who will blink first, the Remington or Tom Lee, since there's not much else to do in this godforsaken shithole, and since they do basically hate each other, as he explains to his glass of whiskey, which needs a number of things explained to it, he has decided. And he smooches the glass, declaring his undying something or other, all the while shooting poison looks at the old Remington, which takes them in stride.

15

ABOUT THE LINDA BURN story, obviously, we could still embellish, so why not go back to her childhood while we're at it, the weeds climbing up the clapboard façade, the shutters that opened onto free, unbound country, fields of vastness awaiting their racing feet, the wind, whose composition could produce in the heart of whoever smelled it, via some mysterious chemistry, the very idea of independence; and the house's half-light, all the secrets it concealed, that it must have concealed, deep within its shadowy bowels.

Everything that went unspoken until it didn't, the parents' conjugal rage, and how she'd slip out to avoid their scene, run all the way into the marshlands, mouth wide open, arms spread, and breathing hard, a little crop duster flying low over the fields. And her wild fabrications that made real situations bearable, her alternative life history full of imaginary characters that lived in the dunes, little friends she'd talk to out loud, who accompanied her everywhere.

Perhaps it was this house she returned to after she'd shut the gate with a clang, marking the caesura between her life with Tom Lee and her life without Tom Lee (the exact transition, a little notch on her timeline, the metallic echo), to go plunge back into the landscape of her early years and search for answers to her questions.

What is it about the connections you have to those natural settings you've known since forever, the ones that, when you return to them after a long time away, restore something ancient and forgotten that you hadn't even realized you'd left behind?

Linda finds these places welcoming. It's true of the house (despite the moldy clapboard siding and peeling paint) and the garden (weedy as ever), and it's also true of the grasslands, in all their utter untidiness, teeming and anxious, at once impoverished and majestic, and the dunes too, and the beach, where she enjoys watching how the sea never seems to give up, how it always comes back with the same spirit and drive, the same energy.

Shouldn't we draw inspiration from this vigor, this vitality, the sheer mass of the wave as it swells, aiming for the shoreline, biting greedily into the beach, a little further up each time, steadily advancing toward its objective, and when it recedes with the low tide, leaves calmly, secure in the notion that it will return, that it will live to fight another day?

There's that, but also the wind's devastating effects, and it's an ambiguous landscape that our Linda is walking through, tenacious yet easily pulverized, for the wind beats against the shore, wrestles with the dunes, eroding their broad shoulders, the protective wall that spares the inlands the wrath of its gusts. In these clashes, the sand is whipped up, the fragile dunes victim of a slow-motion massacre, losing their silhouette, a whole landscape crumbling away, not noticeably from one day to the next, but gradually, inexorably pushed back and flattened by the corrosive action of the wind, one bite at a time. And it is amid this contest between wind and naturally powdery sand, whose quartz grains spiral and lift, carried by the wind that displaces them as it pleases, that our Linda Burn stiffens her body bent against the northwest wind, arms crossed against her belly, thighs battered by the flaps of an old rain slicker, hair having its way with her, slapping against her face, whipping her cheeks and mouth, impeding her vision like a dark blindfold mashed against her eyes, or just the reverse, fleeing her head, zigzagging in the marine air, serpentine vines, kites shunted to and fro, tethered to her scalp; despite all this, she drags herself obstinately forward, into the wind, her features crinkled, tensed against her invisible yet palpable opponent.

What's interesting about this kind of landscape, with its weeds and marine air, the sense of utter abandonment it exudes, left to fend for itself in the sea mists, is that, despite the retreating dunes and the way the wind gradually reconfigures the beach after years of wear, it's much less subject to modification than a cityscape (subjected as it is to the swirl of changing signage, you know what it's like, demolitions and reconstructions, sidewalks widened and streets potholed, all that jackhammering that starts up again with the return of spring, the pulse of life in the city). The bay is spared all that, and facing such permanence, you feel (I'm talking about Linda Burn, of course) that you're back in touch with that little part of yourself that is also—you see where I'm going with this—unchanged, the part you've carried with you everywhere in the great world, concealed, crouching in fear of being exposed, of being altered in the magma of new situations that have been less than kind with it, and now, that dares reawaken in this familiar, unchanged place and emerge from its shell and show itself, the unearthed personality of Linda Burn that opens up like a dehydrated vegetable you've just soaked in water.

And this is what Linda Burn probably comes seeking in this landscape, where the townsfolk like to think she has found refuge after slamming the gate, stuffing her overweight suitcase into the car trunk and turning the ignition, which maybe didn't start right away, the motor wheezing and coughing at first (might we not rightly interpret the motor's sputtering as a form of mild disapproval, a concern that perhaps she hadn't made the right decision, a plea for her to reconsider, an automotive groan in response to her repeated efforts to get the engine to turn over), but which finally did start, and speeding out of town, where she had no more reason to linger.

The landscape continues to roll past Donovan's windshield with a recognizable sameness cut from the same cloth.

Puffy clouds overhead, rising dough with bulging air pockets.

Or, if you'd rather, clean little clouds looking like sterile cotton balls, immaculate compresses wafting across the blue canvas of sky.

Not like European skies, where it's said they're more like disgusting old cotton balls that have already served their purpose.

Further, the circle can be enlarged to include, for instance, Linda Burn's best childhood friend, with whom we can assume she has stayed in contact, a loose kind of contact, you know how it is, they don't see each other for months at a time, or maybe even a year goes by. But every time they do get together, their relationship is redeemed by the times they've already spent in each other's company, and that weigh favorably in the balance of what needs to be renegotiated, changes that each one senses in the other, those fraught ingredients that mix happily into their little cache of shared experience that softens their combined effect.

Is it possible that, instead of withdrawing into the shack by the water all by herself to stare blankly into the mists (which would eventually have the effect of reinvigorating her stultified thoughts if she kept at it every day), Linda might have left Tom's apartment, as we've said, and sought refuge with this old friend? Alternatively, might we not imagine her driving to the town where this girlfriend lives, honking under her window and enjoining her to come stay with her in the shack by the ocean (a text message would have given her enough advance notice to pack her bags and be ready), where they would each sit and take stock of their respective lives, swapping stories that they'd punctuate with provisional conclusions whenever they felt it appropriate to issue some summarizing statement?

Each of them sitting in an armchair by the fireplace, hair still wet from a recent swim in the always too chilly Atlantic waters where they simply had to go for a dip nevertheless, running out of the surf to their beach towels, shivering with cold, returning home to light a fire and picking up their conversation where they'd left off, the inexhaustible topic of their love lives.

Each one in turn goes on endlessly with her personal story, when what they perhaps should have done was to let their memories settle out more naturally, because, in the end, didn't they mix up everything?

You start to believe that there must be some higher gratification in the obscure pleasure of talking about your past relationships, since, at the same time your hasty interpretations are supposed to be shedding light on things, they're in fact muddying the waters, definitively precluding, as far as I can tell, the kind of comprehension that a more inward-looking, more cautious, patient, and secret kind of scrutiny might have had a chance at achieving.

This all happens as if these alterations lost their importance in favor of what takes place in their friendship where this flow of words turns into a cement that pleasantly strengthens its ties.

And speaking of text messages, it crosses Donovan's mind that he'd like to send Jane an SMS, but the idea exits his head as fast as it entered, or if it sticks around and settles in, it does so only as a vague notion, an amorphous plan that would require a few extra conditions—oh, nothing much, just that awful, unbridgeable gap between wish and fulfillment—for him to bring it to fruition.

One wonders whether Linda Burn, after one of these heart-to-hearts with her girlfriend (either her friend advised her to do this, or she herself was getting tired of droning on about missed opportunities and hypotheticals instead of taking the bull by the horns), decided to hop back into her car and drive all the way back to Tom Lee's apartment, a conjecture worth investigating, and finding the door locked shut, no forwarding address, she stands there in the hallway, leans against the wall, slides down to the floor into a squat, and starts to cry, as if it were only now that their true separation had taken effect.

16

It DIDN'T TAKE LONG for the sun to slip out from behind the inconsequential clouds, and now Donovan is driving right into it, struck in the face with an almost unbearable intensity.

He flips down the white leatherette visor, while the little varnished turtle hanging from his rearview mirror sways back and forth (a kind of oscilloscope, if you see what I mean, that registers any jolts made by the car, any lateral movement along the road, what else, maybe the rotation of the earth, the way any pendulum would).

There's Linda Burn's sister, too, whose name comes up with a certain regularity.

She lives with a handsomely rustic brute of a farmer who, so it seems, leaves her every so often to go spend a few days in town where he says he has business to attend to.

After a while, she fell into the habit of taking a lover whenever her handsome farmer would head for town, usually from among the seasonal workers. These lovers provide consolation to keep her mind off her husband's absences. And when the seasonal workers depart, when they pick up and move on, it's the husband's turn to console her, that she might take her mind off her absent lovers.

And that's how life goes with Linda Burn's sister, who misses her husband in the arms of her lovers, and misses her lovers in her husband's arms, and so on (since no one can do without nostalgia, or so Linda Burn's sister thinks).

The visor isn't doing the trick, so Donovan digs blindly into the glove compartment, feeling around while keeping his eyes on the road, his body leaning toward the right, allowing his seatbelt to slip a bit, while he searches for his sunglasses, sightlessly interpreting each object he fondles until his hand comes upon the soft rectangular silicone sleeve, open at one end.

Maybe the specter of the sister, or that of the handsome brute of a farmer (in the bar, they're squinting with that look, how to describe it, of someone who draws in customers using vaguely underhanded methods) is in the back of Linda's mind, because if she got into her car with all her belongings and took to the road on that day she first met Tom Lee (see how they ensnare you with their sleazy scenarios), if she was so quick to follow Tom, so available, so unhampered by anything, doesn't it seem likely she was running away from something (they ask, lowering their voice), shouldn't we consider the possibility that (now they've got that look in their eyes again) the handsome brute of a farmer started going after his own sister-in-law, propositioning her in ways she couldn't accept?

Linda Burn, her arm still red from the farmer's palm that had closed around it like a pincer so that she'd give in, having struggled to break free, had jumped into the car (after going up to get her bag, which she probably stuffed helter-skelter, forgetting whatever) and drove without thinking, straight ahead, stopping only at that gas station when she saw that the gas gauge needle was pointing dangerously to the red zone.

There was no shortage of absurdly speculative versions of the story, but some more amusing ones as well, like the version where Linda Burn (puffing on a cigarette, sitting in front of her beach house, her affair with Tom Lee having been so thoroughly processed in the grinder of confidences as to become all but unrecognizable, leaving nothing but piles of crumbs forming all around her, a hodgepodge, the whole thing reduced to rubble, shattered into a thousand pieces by the power of well-intentioned words; and she now realizes that the down-and-dirty true confession approach had devastated these important episodes of her private life, that, short of keeping them all to herself, she should have processed them in a more respectful and circumspect manner), after putting out her cigarette against the stone door frame, gathers her car keys and her clothes, and sets off to get back together with Tom Lee—at least, that's her intention.

Because, when she rings the doorbell to his apartment (with her suitcase at her feet, the same soft travel bag where she stuffs her things every time she leaves a place), a young woman opens up, whom Linda at first mistakes for his new girlfriend, an understandable misapprehension, and immediately begins to assess her every feature, with every positive trait she observes feeling like a knife in her gut, and the negative ones as well, but for other reasons. The woman in question, showing no particular emotion, simply waits politely for an explanation as to why this stranger has rung her doorbell on this early evening, perhaps a little annoyed by Linda's weary expression, which she has no way of interpreting, and consequently, no way to defuse.

It's the new tenant, Linda will eventually learn after a stammering, feverish exchange, Linda, limp as a dishrag from all the emotion, hardly able to stand on her feet, finally invited to come in, please sit down, let me get you some coffee, and is served a mug of dishwater. And soon they're talking as if they'd known each other all their lives, sitting on the couch, the new tenant crossing one leg over the other, the point of her right pump against her left ankle, a sophisticated pose, and Linda, still a little dazed and slumping, slowly recovers her strength and sits a little straighter, while the tenant grows more relaxed, drops the formality, so that each progressively assumes the position of the other, as they reach out in the other's direction.

Elizabeth James (the new tenant) had moved in only a few days before and knew hardly anyone in that still enigmatic and confusing town, whose grid pattern she could see from her living room window with its orthogonal mullions repeating the same checkerboard pattern. Three somewhat distant coworkers (she had moved there for her job) and the two morning-shift employees at the local McDonald's (a woman and a young man), where she went for breakfast (she dipped her hash browns in ketchup while looking out the window at the merry-go-round of cars on the traffic circle) were the only human beings with whom she had any social contact since her arrival. Understandably then, she was more than glad to offer some coffee to a young woman her own age, who might well have been a friend, or even make her dinner, which is in fact what happened.

And this is how Linda came to take her evening meal with a stranger in the former apartment of Tom Lee where she herself had lived, where only the bibelots had changed, three little statues and a few framed photographs that Elizabeth had placed here and there, and which presented a segmented panorama of her life, how her body had evolved, people who had shown her affection. She chewed, a bit dazed by all the visual data, so Elizabeth, also chewing, walked her through the photos, pointing to each and commenting, talking with her mouth full, I'm seven in that one over there; and Linda gazed at the little girl who no longer existed, with her blond curls, her plaid dress on her shapeless body, and you felt like crying, because no one would ever, ever see her again for real, this little girl with that smile, those baby teeth, those curls, a little body that didn't look like much, no one ever again, and it came as an awful revelation.

And so on and so forth, the whole gallery, the cousin, the sister, the first husband, the coworkers that Elizabeth James had left behind in another city, brought together for a group shot, mugging for the camera, one of them appearing alone in a different photo, a big smile across his face that you didn't know quite how to interpret. Paul, Elizabeth explained, as if his first name provided the key to the mystery.

Paul was wearing a mustard-colored shirt with an illegible logo, with some sort of sports field in the background, and maybe a little creek off to one side, muddy water running behind a fringe of tall grasses.

You must be exhausted, and you didn't get a hotel room, so why don't you stay here for the night, Elizabeth James offered, you know where everything is; and you can only imagine Linda curled up uncomfortably on the couch where she may well have ended up on certain nights in the past, when the urge for solitude tore her from her shared bed, or some disagreement, an entirely harmless discussion that had taken a wrong turn, a vague feeling of discontentment that was best left unnamed, going to fall back to sleep there in the living room at dawn that was already piercing holes in the crooked blinds, sunbeams that dotted the opposite wall with a thousand points of light that seemed to belong there, unpretentious and gentle, lulling her to sleep.

There was obviously all manner of speculation as to what went on when Linda Burn spent the night in the apartment now being rented by Elizabeth James.

The uncomfortable couch, and how the remains of the day's emotions were still banging around in her head, caring little for her need to sleep, did Linda go knocking on Elizabeth's door? Or was it Elizabeth James who, walking past Linda on tiptoe on her way to the bathroom, noticed that she wasn't asleep, and approached the couch? Whatever the case, she may well have given Linda a big hug to calm her down, it's okay, it's okay, and Linda cuddling, not wanting to stop, while the other whispers her lullabies, rocking her gently, there now, everything's all right, all right, drawing out the syllables to produce a calming effect, softly stroking Linda's hair and face. Did they go any further than that? Entirely up to you. But no one is keeping you from imagining, if it tickles your fancy, a few bolder moves on the part of Elizabeth James in the bedroom formerly occupied by Tom Lee, toward an appreciative Linda Burn, who welcomed them, for want of anything better, because someone was taking care of her at least. On certain evenings, the townsfolk lower their voices, and with a gleam in their eye that shines even brighter than those already gleaming, steer the imagination of the newcomer in that direction, before washing their hands of any responsibility.

The young man who worked at the McDonald's (one of the rare humans, you'll recall, with whom Elizabeth James had spoken since her arrival) was named, I might as well tell you right away, Rick Barnett Junior—or Rick Sunville, depending on the version.

He's the one who took their order the next morning when they went to wolf down their breakfast across from the traffic circle before parting ways, each returning to her respective life.

Rick had, shall we say, all the best attributes of youth, in particular his laugh, the kind you'd find obnoxious in most people, but in him, as in any other good-looking young man, it didn't seem to imply he was stupid, the way such crude, throaty resonance often does, but rather, it sounded like youth itself, with all its uncertainty, its capacity to find fun in everything, the mix of fear and exultation that was audible in its every note, the difficulty of being in the present moment, a nasty childhood

whose echo you could detect in its arpeggios, the whole story
of his life so far, even the history of youth itself, all trembling in
that laughter, his sexual experience still so green, his pleasure in
things not yet quite under control, the inhaled smoke, the beers
that ease you into late-night conversation, pale dawn as you
head for home, the myriad futures whose little multi-colored
glass crystals you hear kaleidoscopically clicking into place as
you gaze down the tube, that clicking sound is also present in
his laugh. That's how I'd describe it, anyway.

He'd been rummaging around behind the counter a while by
the time Linda, who'd taken her tray and found a table, became
aware of his existence, checking him out on the sly (or simply
from behind the haze that always inserts itself between you and
the rest of the world in the early morning), noting his build
and features. With so few customers at that hour, he was free
to leave his work space and go stand in proximity to the two
young women, using the excuse of seeing "if everything is okay."
Everything was, but that didn't mark the end of their exchange;
rather, it was the conversation starter that launched him into
a freewheeling narration of his recent hiring, where he slipped
in just enough pieces of personal information to flesh out a
persona, enough of a life of his own to appear to be someone
in their eyes, as the slanted rays of morning light poured into
the fast food interior, better sculpting his physique than had the
flourescent tubes behind the counter.

They lingered in conversation, to the rhythm of noisy
chewing and swallowing, licking of fingers, rustling of paper
napkins and containers, the soundtrack of your typical breakfast
under the golden arches in an American city, while outside the
glass enclosure, cars were bumper to bumper on the traffic
circle, peeling off at the desired thoroughfare, beating around
the bush, so to speak, before heading off to their intended
destination.

No traffic circles for Donovan, who was still on his rectilinear trajectory, that single ribbon of highway extending all the way to the mountainous horizon that seems to forever recede before him.

Through the smoky lenses of his sunglasses, the world is a sepia wash, a faded version of itself, like decaying film stock from the nineteen seventies.

The boy at the McDonald's counter had a cheery disposition (even if he had to keep a lid on his store of not-so-happy secrets that must have come to visit, arriving in motley gangs on sleepless nights, like little sorrows you'd hoped to have put behind you, but which are revived at the midnight hour, all hale and hearty with their renewed vigor, preening and pestering you to pay attention to them, all swagger and itching to cross swords in the wee hours). He lived in a tiny one-room apartment that did, nevertheless, have the one advantage (he explained to them as they finished their tart orange juice so full of fiber that they had a hard time believing it was only pulp, as it left what felt like flakes of blotter paper on their tongues) of being located close to work, and where (Linda would soon get the chance to verify this firsthand) he had thumbtacked a large piece of navy blue fabric as a makeshift curtain, just gauzy enough to allow the city lights to twinkle through.

Was it that same night or the next that Rick got a bad case of the willies when Linda agreed to follow him home to this room, just a few blocks from the burger joint where he worked, not in the direction of the traffic circle (in that direction, the city very quickly morphed into a complex weave of roadways before melting into a no-man's-land that was anything but urban: most of the roads eventually crossed the wide river to go innervate the nether shore where, once past the warehouse district, they soon plunged into the patchwork of farm fields in every shade of green, beige, and brown where nothing stood between you and the horizon line), but in the opposite direction. If you turn left as you leave through the glass doors of the restaurant, stay on the same sidewalk, cross two streets, and when you get to Booth, it's pretty simple, you just turn left again and you're there, a few steps away, at number 32; Rick punches in the door code and turns to Linda's upturned face.

What's going on in Rick's smile at this moment is something that really needs to be accurately described. Because here's what's happening: he's smiling, and like all smiles, it looks like it's expressing joy of some kind, while at the same time betraying a hint of panic. It's the first available refuge for his panic to shelter in, it's the form his panic assumes, the form that something not far from true distress has spontaneously chosen to mask its true nature. In this use of the smile, which is somewhat at cross-purposes with the standard use, we don't read a simple contentment, as one would ordinarily, a gratification unafraid to display itself, a serene signal sent to the other of the well-being we're experiencing, and that we owe largely to that same other, a kind of sweet delight we can't hide, for which we might even express thanks. This smile, on the contrary, is the product of a sudden discomfort. A deep unease that resorts to this paradoxical outlet, an unsettling emotion that the smile is attempting to expel; the smile of an anxious young man who isn't handling the situation very well, and who is countering what he believes to be the certainties of the other (which, to some degree, feel to him like aggression) with this fragile, crumbling rampart.

But the other, of course, isn't nearly as self-assured as he thinks, and as Linda gazes up toward him (Rick's hand leaves the entry system keypad and moves blindly to the door and gives it a push), one could discern much contradictory data all jockeying for first place, while desire attempts to push ahead of the unruly crowd and silence all competitors. And desire succeeds, in the end, in gagging all other considerations, one by one, finally escorting Linda and Rick into his mansard with the blue linen curtain.

Donovan glances at the rearview mirror, if only to maintain some semblance of the careful driver, but he highly doubts that anything will be making an appearance in its rectangle, which offers nothing to the eye but a perfectly mineral backward tracking shot, a big wide angle, in cinemascope even, where you recognize all the tropes from famous Westerns, though there's no one on horseback to lend any intensity to the scene, and at least for the moment, no other vehicle on the road at all.

17

WHAT HAPPENED THE FIRST time in the young man's room, well yes, I'm going to tell you, actually.

They've drunk quite a bit, a bottle of California red that Rick removed from a little cupboard under the sink, and at the precise moment that interests you, Linda is sitting on Rick, (who is stretched out on the bed, his feet on the pillow and his head at the foot of the bed, I hope you're getting the picture). They're moving together in rhythm, one inside the other, smiling. What's original about the scene is that Linda is still holding her wineglass, which she brings to her lips from time to time (the tannins take on a special texture, as if enriched and multiplied, in contact with her mouth). She continues to hold the wineglass like a scepter (Hey, careful you don't spill it, okay? says Rick), concentrating her attention on its cool stem which she pinches between her fingers, struggling to keep the rising sensation of pleasure from overwhelming her, to prevent what's happening in her sex and irradiating throughout her whole body, legs and arms, and yes, even the hand holding the glass, from loosening her grip and letting the glass fall to the floor, it's an important piece in a complex machine that she has to keep in balance, the glass acting like a piston invisibly connected to the rest, and she moves it up and down in the air, holding it perfectly level, trying to focus all her attention on her fingertips, but then, Oops, sorry, I'm coming.

It is in this top-floor room that Rick opened up to Linda Burn, night after night, revealing bits of his personal story, as did Linda in turn, the house in the dunes, moving in with her married sister (named Norma) and her rustic brute of a farmer husband, her escape, meeting Tom Lee at the gas station, and everything that ensued, when she moved in with him, the day she up and left, the return to her childhood home, and then, the day she got the urge to come back, the obvious need to get back together that seemed so crystal clear in her head, but which came up against the abandoned apartment now occupied by someone else, Elizabeth James, whom you saw with me at McDonald's that first morning, and everything else that we've already learned, including the scene of their first encounter, which Rick was always wanting her to repeat, the kind of scene that people starting relationships love to rehash, each asking the other what they were thinking at the time, the whole film in shot/counter-shot, and what were you thinking to yourself at that point? And what about then? Rick would ask her to reprise the narrative, generally while he was running something over her body (anything, his finger, his lips, his dick, a feather that happened to be there, a piece of fabric, a leather glove he'd hold at the wrist, sections of a mandarin orange he'd eat off her one by one), and what were you thinking when I came out from behind the counter and walked over to where you were sitting (and let's not even mention, if you please, the time he drizzled over her a whole bottle of maple syrup that turned the bed into a sticky mess). And Linda would answer that she knew immediately, that she didn't have to make it happen, not even try to seem nicer (or meaner), when he came over to chat with them. It was meant to happen, and it did, Rick stood there by the window, looking out on the merry-go-round of cars on the traffic circle that moved as if this was the way the world was intended to proceed, and he asked them if everything was all right, the bacon and all that, and she understood in an instant, she knew that this question was just the tip of the iceberg, that there was something massive below.

This wasn't just a well-trained worker making nice with the customers either (and while he was being so professional, toss a couple of ego chips onto the gaming table just to test what he could arouse in the other's eyes); and it wasn't even one of those trick questions that's looking for an opening, so that when asked if everything is all right, you understand it's you and me, babe, and I know you know what I mean. Rather, it was as if he also knew that there was only one way this story could go, and he evaluated this conclusion with a cool head, the way you might read highly accurate meteorological data.

He stayed there in front of the window, talking with them about this and that, saying a few things about his life, where he lived, expanding their acquaintance, but it was a done deal, like it or not, they were going to hook up, for as long as Linda chose to stay in town—stop it, that tickles.

Everything they were experiencing together, a fate already sealed that morning at the fast food restaurant, everything they foretold, now coming to pass, this thing they built and nurtured night after night, the sum total of all the moments spent together, would somehow or other amount to a relationship.

And the way Rick took her was so different from how Tom Lee did it, you almost needed a totally different verb to designate it.

Even kissing, at this stage, felt like a wholly different activity.

Rick, in case you're interested, was boldly invasive right off the bat, thrusting his probe-like tongue down your throat, braced for action, a kind of advance publicity for the marvels awaiting you. While our Tom, much more labial, if you get my meaning, would nip and lightly bite, more playful and sophisticated, less interested in the shock troop intervention, more apt to dawdle.

Linda and Rick got into the habit of meeting up at the Winner Bar, a narrow little café, nothing special, the kind that made you wonder how it could live up to its name.

Words got lost in the hubbub, you had to practically shout to make yourself heard, diluting what they could confide in the physical effort of straining the voice. Linda had the impression that by talking louder, she simplified her ideas, as if there were some inversely proportional relation at work: the lower you spoke, the richer your point, but when you spoke up, your content automatically became more schematic, as if the thinness of what you were conveying might fit more easily into the other's ear canal.

Rick seemed like a fish in water, drinking his beers in the low glow of improvised neon lighting, not to mention a low ceiling painted the color of spinach that seemed to absorb the little light there was. And yet his face always seemed perfectly lit, as if a lighting director on set had arranged all the projectors in such a way as to highlight his face only, setting him apart from the rest of the cast who were drinking and talking just like him, but whose faces faded into the indistinct and noisy mass of bar regulars. And the same went for their dialogue, almost all of which took place outside the capture range of the mic, which the boomer was undoubtedly assigned to suspend right over Rick's head, apart from a few random phrases extracted from the general din, a sampling meant to alternate between anecdotes and statements of truth. From various incidents that involved you, a general philosophy could be drawn, which would then solicit further illustrations, once the principles were laid down, which would seem to corroborate the theory. The interest of this operation was fairly obvious, that is, the re-sequencing inside of one's self of what seemed at first a total mess, and which was now given a respectable, communicable form.

After they had had a few beers at the Winner (the place was managed by a certain Clayton Craig, himself the subject of much tongue-wagging, but if I launch into his story, I'll never get back to this one, because Clayton Craig deserves a novel all to himself), just enough time to gauge that night's trends (basically, to conclude that nothing had really changed, that it was still a stewpot of messy lives, that, with the help of a little alcohol, the regulars still displayed that curious propensity to rationalize, to see things more clearly even as their thoughts grew cloudier, that mad desire to apply grids to unstable, shifting categories, to chase after slippery concepts, and when they failed to nail down anything concrete, to retreat and return, digging further, rattling off the same arguments as before in the hope of finding something they hadn't seen the first time around), our two lovebirds went back to Rick's room, where he would jump up onto the bed and, standing on the mattress without even taking off his Nikes, he would sing to Linda, "I'm the guy," a parodied version of Roberta Flack's "I'm the Girl," where she says she knows she'll always be number two (how else to say it, a supporting role, a plan B), and she's okay with that.

We can imagine what Rick's days are like, wiping down the counter, slipping on his latex gloves and piling the bacon, cheese, and beef patties on their buns, working the cash register, pointing his index finger at the proper key after twirling it in the air a few times, as if searching for the right landing strip, accompanying the gesture with a drawn out syllable or two, the hum of the circling plane's engine, all of which provides the customer a temporary distraction from the cashier's hesitation, but at the same time, a sign that he's being attended to, that he needn't interfere so long as the twirling and the humming continue.

Or perhaps, during off-peak hours, he stands by the window and watches the cars on the traffic circle performing their relentless urban spectacle out there on the other side of the glass.

When clouds gather and it starts to sprinkle, the pavement glistens and the cars are shiny colorful hard candies.

And all those refreshed and brilliant colors must somehow

make their way to Rick's retina, nicely filtered by the plate-glass window, screened by the droplets, sometimes clinging to the glass, immobile and adhesive, cohesive molecules holding on with the same unbelievable sticking power as certain shellfish, glued to the glass whose verticality hardly offers the ideal refuge, defying the laws of gravity, stubbornly globular, and other times breaking free and sliding down, leaving behind a streak, a path, creating oblique stripes down the side of the plate glass, or here and there, a burst of wind or some other rule of physics cause to make a right angle, into which other droplets follow, as if to take advantage of a fresh opening, drawn to it somehow, the droplets swim like spawning fish up a river, or like tadpoles, if you prefer, wriggling along, swiftly propelled through the rivulet.

What thoughts go through one's head before such a spectacle, how does the amorphous shape of a personal life get reconfigured in the mind of someone gazing at the soothing tableau of shiny candy-colored cars in rotation behind the weft of raindrops that weave their movable canvas against the glass? What sort of memories does it conjure up, which previously lived moments get restored wholesale, what little chunk of stratified time, mostly from his childhood, he guesses, whenever he gets absorbed in contemplating the journey of raindrops down the plate-glass window?

He wipes down the counter with a damp cloth.

In the seating section, a few rain-soaked customers reflexively hunch over their trays, attempting to retract from their wet clothing, as if to buffer their skin from its clammy contact.

Rick gets it into his head that he's watching over them somehow, that he has offered them this haven from the rain, they who sought shelter in the nearest grotto, these companions of Ulysses, chewing on their food in this temporary lair, escapees from a storm at sea. And as he listens to them chewing, he wonders what role he'd like to play in this story, whether he should be the scheming Cyclops, or why not Circe, who's hardly any better, for you can just see their faces sprouting snouts that will soon be rooting through the garbage on their messy trays, greasy French fry rejects, limp lettuce, bits of onion dropped from hamburgers, all congealing in a mishmash of ketchup and mustard, creating the effect of a second-tier drip painting; or maybe Calypso, more even-tempered, concerned only with her own pleasure, that's the way she's most often imagined anyway, her trysts behind the blue linen fabric thumbtacked across the window; and his Ulysses named Linda, undoubtedly in the process of repairing her raft at this very moment, preparing for her impending departure in a couple of days, what could he do to hold her back, and the rain continues to whip the window, and the cars pursue their rondo, the customers' damp clothing gives the seating area a certain odor that mixes with the smell of grease and hot oil, the sky is gray and luminous, silvery, it's an Oklahoma City fast food moment, experienced by a young man who works there, one rainy day, a young man who met a young woman a little older than he is (she'd come back to this city to hook back up with a man she'd left, who then saw fit, after all that had happened, to vanish) and with whom he'd had a brief fling, in this season of alternating heat and rain, and he wipes the plastic-coated counter with a rag, half daydreaming, his head a box full of sweets from these recent days, bits and pieces of his childhood, and unedited plans for assorted futures.

This short affair with Rick would leave a tender, harmonious trace in Linda Burn's mind. Not quite enough to compensate for failing to see Tom Lee again, she wasn't about to trade one story for the other, but it would lighten the burden as she moved forward in time.

Yes, Linda Burn would put the city behind, leaving the two apartments she'd spent time in to fend for themselves, the one where Tom used to live, now occupied by Ms. James and the photograph of Paul in the mustard-yellow shirt that reigns from atop the mantelpiece, and Rick's mansard, with the unforgettable weave of the blue linen drape.

She would be leaving the city, but the thought of Rick would continue to pleasantly enfold her, a balm to her soul that would keep working its magic long after she ceased to apply it.

The memory of time spent with Rick would act as a comfy divider between herself and the world, a soft wall, inflatable, an invisible Michelin Man suit, maybe you've been there at some point, against which all the little daily aggressions simply bounce off, leaving you unscathed.

So, dressed in her shockproof outerwear, Linda walks the highways and byways with a lively, happy step (or almost).

18

You might say that Tom Lee's move to the ranch was a real boon for the folks in the nearby town, for they now have a pretty clear idea not only of his reasons for moving there, but of all the individuals surrounding Linda Burn, and taken together, the characters of this little saga compose something like a deck of cards for the boys at the bar (raging against the coming twilight with beer upon beer, tall tale after even taller tale), who shuffle and draw at random, coming up with this or that protagonist, and then tell his or her story to anyone within earshot, a story with many missing pieces, many dark corners where they switch on their flashlights and show you around, narrating each episode with an air of mystery in their voices, eyes squinting, voice softened, until all of a sudden, they reveal one of the darker areas and shine upon it the light of their particular truth.

But that's not all.

On the topic of Linda Burn's brother-in-law, for example, they now have some real doozies that they've been collecting for quite a while, most of which have to do with his escapades in town, though some go back much further, and feature an authoritarian father (the handsome brute of a farmer's own father, that is), who reigned over his household with a kind of archaic terror that seeped into every corner of every room, altering the chemistry of the air, and that his mere presence would revive.

In the eyes of his close family, there was something imposing about his body that had less to do with his build (a big man, but hardly athletic) than the irrational vigor that emanated from his overall persona. His protruding abdomen, rather than making him look jolly and harmless the way most round bellies do (for they seem to blossom blissfully in a way that puts people immediately at ease), only added to the obscure authority exuded by his entire being. And the steely gaze that his dark eyes (or were they blue, but darkened with the onset of his tempestuous rages) projected before him felt like cannonballs shooting continuously from those two guns, against which no one had any effective defense.

Say what you will, but the presence of a father like him (tyrannical, paunchy, with that murderous look) in a house where you're taking your first steps, that has to leave a mark.

In the little town nearby, just ask and they'll be more than willing to provide a highly detailed description of the farmer's childhood home, the dining room, the red wallpaper, the two or three windows that open outward, English-style, a bay window that juts out into the garden like an aquarium. And the father's massive corpulence, backlit against the window, but filled in somewhat by lamps set around the room (bell-shaped lampshades with fringes that look like plumb lines yielding to the pull of gravity).

Framed by the windows and cut up into a grillwork pattern by mullions, the bits of rectangular landscape form mobile tableaux as you walk across the room, with the father's body always there to block the view, or part of it, as if those landscapes were nothing but an emanation of his person, an extension, a background tailor-made to his silhouette.

The father's body forever inscribed in the landscape, leaving his mark, his imprint, owning it merely by the way he inhabits it.

This too-round, too-paunchy, too-stationary father body, dark and looming against the bright windows, this despotic body must certainly be concealing something, secrets stacked up inside each other like Russian dolls, one or two of which we might like to open and have a peek.

The farmer's father, who was known for bossing his family around, never had to say a word or raise his voice to shout orders, but rather, by the sheer force of his presence, was able to impose the desired discipline that needed constant reaffirmation, readjustment, and reinforcement. This father, as I was saying, was keeping something hidden inside, a painful secret that he must have ruminated when he was alone. And whenever the secret reared its ugly head, when it invaded his thoughts in the form of who-knows-what kind of hideous monster, filthy and slimy (scaly and covered in gristly crests all over its head), he silenced it, paralyzed it through intimidation, he himself remaining rigidly still so as not to upset the container in which he had sealed it up.

Wouldn't that help explain the petrified pater, protected by the backlighting that kept his face in the shadows, a convenient veil to shroud the emotional wreckage that might show in his face, the protruding gut that acted as a cage where his secret was rotting away, the windowless prison where this secret walked in circles, dragging its ball and chain as it paced?

And the farmer, who wasn't yet a farmer then, but a scrawny, snot-nosed ten-year-old, ribs showing through the pale skin of his pathetic little chest with its colorless nipples, ankles caked in mud, and who would get slapped every time he entered the house, a sign that he should probably go clean himself up, though he was never sure, he who had no clear information on which to base anything, did he not sense, without actually perceiving its form, the scaly animal whose head bristling with crests that would occasionally pay him a visit, without introducing itself, a ghostly presence he had no way of identifying, but which left behind muddy tracks where it had passed?

Wasn't that it, then, the weird unpleasantness he felt, the fleeting presence of his father's secret that quickly inspected the son's soul before returning to the prison where it lodged, while the young boy cracked open a few unripe hazelnuts and popped the flat-tasting nut into his mouth, or maybe (because kids are like that too), as he stared at the wings of a butterfly that had landed right in front of him, with their scales that leave powdery traces on your fingers if you happen to touch them, wondering what to do with this proximity to the fragile, mute lepidopteran as it flits anxiously from flower to flower, and which finally opted to light upon the wooden fence and rest, taking stock of the situation and wondering what to do next, without noticing that it had come within range of the boy, whose reactions would naturally be hard to predict—or did it rely on the speed of its reflexes and the quick lightness of its flight to escape the first sign of a move in its direction?

Roadwork ahead, the orange and white cones give fair warning.

Donovan drives past a car dealership with all its vehicles parked outdoors, the sun beating down on their gleaming bodies.

He's behind a truck for several miles, the double yellow line forbidding him to pass. He's tailgating it, wondering what the truck is transporting, what the truck driver is thinking about as he surges ahead into open space, unlike Donovan.

Folks all say that Spencer's childhood home (that's his name, the handsome brute of a farmer) was full of stuffed animal heads mounted on the wall, the spoils of the paternal grandfather's hunting adventures, each one provided with an engraved plaque nailed to the wooden mount indicating the date on which the rifle had bested the beast.

It must have been here among all these trophies that Spencer's father figured out how his body fit in space, and how to wrestle with the boisterous glory of his own father, to deal with the ostentatious display of his hunting skills that had bequeathed to his offspring the nauseating proof of his bravura and acumen, dead animal heads staring into the void with those artificial eyes whose tinted resin was the only clean thing about them, the only thing that hadn't once been alive.

As a child, Spencer would wander from room to room, weighed down by a vague sense of guilt at not having been there to save them.

The most expressive among them were given a name, he'd greet them with a furtive hello in the morning, eyes lowered, shoulders hunched, as if his whole body were apologizing for the previous generations, feeling as though he were bearing the burden of all the sins committed by those who, by transmitting their genes, had handed down the foul-smelling freight of their weaknesses and sundry misdeeds perpetrated over the years. He would go eat his pancakes, thinking of all the prairie grasses these animals might have looked forward to, and that the grandfather hadn't allowed them the time to enjoy. Breakfast was never easy, you had to learn to sit there and chew in front of them, and learn to find pleasure in the raspberry syrup-soaked stack.

The child Spencer would grow bolder as the day progressed. He'd talk softly at first, as if the busts required appeasement, as if you had to keep nursing the trauma of their final moments, the scene of violence where it all culminated—the chase, the feel of tall foliage against their shanks, the wind in their muzzles, the wide woolen blanket of sky above, and all the other ingredients that went into being alive—ending in a senseless bloodbath, because of a momentary lapse of attention, a split second of foolish trust in the beauty of the world.

And then, after a display of all the empathy you could muster (as if by doing so, in the consolation expressed to them, he would be cleansing himself of all the vestiges of shame left upon him by these incidents), he would adopt the other point of view, that of his grandfather, and seek to show them that he, too, had reasons for doing what he did.

And since he felt some resistance on their part to the hunter's point of view he was now espousing, that's when things tipped toward a feeling he couldn't quite handle.

He would take a hard line, and find that the deer, the fox, the coyote were all imbeciles for their inability to broaden their vision to include something other than their idiotic little selves, for stewing away in their resentment and the mute accusations he had to face every morning when he got up, every hour of the day when his gaze would meet one of theirs, that unequivocal resinous stare that sprang from a single idea, that of victimhood, displayed there as incontrovertible proof of the grandfather's cruelty, and the awful responsibility handed down to his descendants.

Is it possible, Spencer thought confusedly, that any victim unable at some point to espouse his torturer's viewpoint will develop the propensity to torture his former torturer? For this is precisely what happened to these heads, in motionless agitation, in soundless protestation, making life miserable for the boy.

So he told them that his grandfather most probably acted blindly, and knew nothing about who they were, but that, if he had known, he still would have blown them away, loading the cartridges into his rifle in the moist morning air and pulling the trigger, and they would be getting just what they deserved, the fractious tribunal, the vicious horde, that left the child not a moment's peace, always making him feel like he'd played a part in all this, simply because he belonged to the tribe of pancake eaters and not to the prairie grazers.

Spencer had come to hate them, and in doing so, developed the brutal personality for which he came to be known. And the fault lies squarely on those stuffed heads, I'm here to tell you.

The heat distorts the shape of the road, making it wavy, or crenelated, irregular, in any case. The sun is an evil genie that gives you a fake version of the landscape, twisted and transformed. Donovan is driving through this heat-altered world where straight lines begin to curl, as if the flat prairie, the mountains, even the sky, were part of a submersible stage set dunked into a gigantic aquarium.

Getting back to Spencer's father, his composed steadiness was the way he'd found to distinguish himself from his own father, who used to parade around beneath his hunting trophies in a permanent victory march. His strategy consisted of pretending that these taxidermy specimens were nothing but decorative objects, ornamental and harmless, just like the wall hangings and ornate curtain tie-backs, the oil paintings representing scenes from the construction of the first railroads, or evenings by the campfire out in the arid lands that typified the country around there.

What mattered for the father was to make his own body the focal point of the household he had founded, and the way he'd found for achieving that was to use the backlighting of the windows, to stand there in front of the room's light source, in all his corpulence, using the strength of his massive contour, the opacity of his blocky build, to express the idea of authority that he sought to impress upon their malleable minds.

His own immobility acted as a way to halt all movement around him, to make his home a stable universe inside which everything knew its place, projecting an image of how the world should be, an orderly thing in which each event occurs in its assigned slot, never chaotic, never leavened by the kind of uncertainty that can so swiftly destroy a life if you're not careful.

19

O'Johnson, Spencer O'Johnson, may I introduce myself, he whispered into Norma's ear as he held her in his arms at the dance, beneath the garlands of flowers and lights, and that's the name she murmured later on, at the house, while they were sewing her dress.

For this is how Norma Burn met Spencer O'Johnson, at a dance, and that's a fact, they'll tell you, beer mug in hand, one of those evening entertainments with a little band, held in the dingy old town ballroom, where bodies press together and come apart in the livid glare, softened only a tad by red and blue lanterns, where a little courtyard allowed guests to get some air when the hall felt too stuffy, when you preferred to hear the music from a distance, with the canopy of navy blue sky overhead.

It was Norma's first dance, and for that matter, the first man to ever hold her in his arms, and she'd decided that he was the real thing, one hand on her lower back, the other holding hers, and with the sheer force of his arm, his hand, his gaze, spun her around just like he was supposed to, so that the outcome of this dance appeared crystal-clear to all in attendance. And even those who had been attracted to Norma when she first walked into the hall had to concede to the obvious.

Even now, when he would take her in bed, there was an inevitability that united them, even when the memory of other bodies slipped between them, those intermittent trysts,

the mistress in town, the seasonal worker, whose ghosts made
their gestures feel a little awkward, because of the need to make
adjustments, but also brought them closer, because of how
quickly they were able to re-adapt, a special something that
suddenly fused them in sweat and movement.

But when they found themselves face to face across the dinner
table, the puppet Norma that Spencer imagined (and who bore
little resemblance to the real one) sat between them and took
up all the room, making it hard for Norma, the real one, to
breathe, sucking up all the oxygen, stifling her speech. And so
Norma simply curled up and disappeared.

Because I haven't mentioned yet that Spencer O'Johnson
had an opinion about everything. He was the kind that would
stick to his guns come hell or high water, and no amount of
reality-checking could change his mind. Here's one of the
unfortunate effects of this intransigence. Whenever Norma
found herself in her husband's field of vision, she felt as if he'd
formed a definitive idea about who she was, the way he did for
everything, and that this preconceived idea would always take
precedence over the tentative little person inside her.

She could have painted herself blue and howled all night
at the moon, or run naked through the fields, his idea of
her would have stayed exactly the same. Well, maybe they're
exaggerating a bit (naked in the fields, he would probably have
shot her dead, and he wouldn't have much liked her howling at
the moon either). But her innermost drives and complexities,
her secret feelings, anything spontaneous and improvised, all of
that went so far over his head that Norma felt nullified by his
blindness. And the little wife he wished she had resembled, the
one he believed in, or pretended to believe in, is the one that
she, in turn, pretended to be, in spite of herself, every time she
was in his presence, for it was the only way to deal with that
level of pigheadedness.

The ideal Norma came between the two spouses, inserting an opaqueness that concealed the real Norma from her husband's view, his gaze stopping at the creature he had completely fabricated, and whom he called Norma, yes, but who had so little to do with the real one who was sealed up in her man's stubborn incomprehension, who was fading away within the prison walls that his incomprehension had manufactured and continued to churn out with all the self-assuredness of a cement mixer that rotates on itself, oblivious to the world.

The creature the husband called Norma was the real Norma's evil twin, and they could not have been more different if they had tried, take it from me.

And Norma's striped bathrobe (the red, blue, green, yellow, pink, and orange stripes followed each other in a seemingly random order) wrapped around the wounded little creature that from inside herself was called Norma, but also around the other one, the wife that Spencer saw and called Norma too, with so much conviction that Norma wasn't quite sure, in the end, who was who.

It's always been an open question as to whether there exists a true version of ourselves, and even seen from inside, where we think we know ourselves best, where we sense subcurrents, our real intentions, our deepest affection, we can't actually define that person in any exhaustive and precise manner. But when you're getting pressured all day long by a phantom version of yourself that the other displays as a scare tactic, you'd have every right to weaken, wouldn't you? Spencer's smug self-assurance was so unshakeable that Norma sometimes wondered which of the two she really was, and experienced the fleeting sense that she corresponded more to his image of her, all the while knowing how wrong it was. People do have this power, don't they, to project a false image of who you are, and their certainty is such that, when you find yourself face to face with them, you yield momentarily to their vision and conform to their pathetic

distortion, against your better judgment, playing the good
soldier, compliant, deprived of all initiative or free will.

You couldn't blame her for wanting to go sit on her stone stoop
and pull herself together, have a smoke and allow what was
buried inside her to surface, something belonging to her alone.

It was her favorite place (not unlike her sister Linda, in the
midst of a breakup) to sit and daydream, to take stock of her
life, to pick up the pieces and put them back together.

When Spencer would leave for a few days, and she was back
from one of her rolls in the hay, she'd sit there and smoke,
allowing all sorts of contradictory sensations to wash over her
like waves.

She felt like a beach, yes, she was that great stretch of
sand battered relentlessly by waves, advancing and retreating,
reconfiguring her, their plaything, however they wished.

Perhaps she was thinking of the house in the dunes, of the
spectacle of the sea when she used to gaze at it for hours.

When they were little, she and Linda used to sit out there
facing the water and tell tales of their forebears emerging on the
horizon, dazed from months of ocean spray and confinement,
so accustomed to the roll of the sea that the too-stable land
seemed to give way beneath their feet.

The ships were at first nothing but specks on the horizon
(two or three dark, condensed droplets whose active ingredients
were about to be released), and out of these molecules emerged
disaster. Slaughter, the ravages of alcohol like some chemical
weapon, and disease, its biological counterpart, against which
the locals possessed no antibodies, unlike the invaders (the
extraterrestrials, whose arrival you breathlessly await, will be no
different, with their shiny space vessels, extraordinary physiques,
and panoply of equipment, or in a more likely scenario, a space

probe that will bring back tiny new life forms that will, of course, prove contaminating).

Inside these minuscule points on the horizon that morphed into enormous hulls topped by ragged sails, there surely had to be an individual, no better or worse than the others, who watched the shoreline draw nearer, never imagining that one day, on these same dunes, his descendants, Linda and Norma Burn, would be sitting on the sand, a rendezvous with their own history.

And what about him, what did this foul-smelling voyager leave behind, clothing stuck to his body with sweat and spume, what thoughts occupied his mind on this journey, those nights in the doldrums, leaning against the railing, cloaked in the star-studded blue of night like a wool blanket pierced by a thousand cigarette burns, their embers still visibly glowing?

He came ashore and set foot on this beach, and it was as if he'd left behind a presence, something that remained in suspension, like the salty air and the wind-whipped sand. For the two women, he was an ethereal, spectral godfather, and they'd confide in him aloud, calling on him to bear witness, sure of the unconditional kindliness of the ancestor, who would think of them as extensions of himself.

Even the sea seemed swept up in a surge of nostalgia for the old world where the ancestor had originated, yielding to the magnetic pull toward the homeland; and then it returned, reproducing the scene of their arrival on land, reaching the shore as they had done.

Foaming and exhausted, this ocean flopped onto the sand around Linda and Norma's feet, much like the dazed crew that must have fallen to their knees there in the sand, saliva on their lips, at the feet of their two descendants.

Norma Burn, wife of O'Johnson, continued to sit there on the stoop smoking and accumulating experiences, while little clouds of tobacco, combusted and consumed, floated across space, hovering above the barnyard in shape-shifting puffs, disappearing the more they moved, melting into the air that finally rendered them invisible.

One puff for the body electric, another puff for self-loathing, and still another for the one who's gone, one for jealousy, and one more for the thrill of the new, the feeling of being alive, and yet so dead, yielding to the ebb and flow of these shifting, changeable impressions.

It was especially true in the summer, when the sky could change so unbelievably from one hour to the next, when the texture of the air was never the same.

A single day could bring insane heat, soaking rains, and significant wind events that ushered in some cooling relief, and all of that in no particular order. Huge temperature swings were not uncommon, and the variations undermined your trust. You could never settle into a stable frame of mind. Even one day without any sudden shift, by that measure, would have seemed like an eternity.

Norma found the unpredictability of it all quite thrilling, and the tyranny of weather delighted her no end. You were constantly being reminded of what it was doing outside, what tricks it had up its sleeve, so that weather became a tangible, living thing that made you feel extra-alive.

There was something in those incessant shifts in the sky's physiognomy that shook you out of an otherwise complacent existence, had the summer been perfectly uniform, like some you've experienced in the past. It's as if the outdoors had decided to strike up a conversation with you, to constantly interact, solicit your attention, remind you of its presence by surrounding your body with its physicality (and the confines of the farm were immediately transcended by these wild swings).

Norma sweat through the heat of the day, her mind awash

in the heightened thought of summer. She watched with joy as catastrophic storms played out on the other side of the windowpane, banging on the sky's stretched skin, drum rolls tearing through the ether. She loved getting caught in the rain as she crossed the barnyard.

Her psychic state reflected these unstable summers, changeable, stormy, intense, and in flux.

Such sensations were like a team of horses hitched together with each one trying to move in a different direction, so that it was impossible to steer or stay on track.

In short, the weather was fickle, and that was just fine, because so are we, changeable like the weather, as they say, and that's the best sign that we're still alive.

When the snows came, that was a whole other story.

Norma and Spencer had to be self-sufficient and resourceful, a few outdoor chores for him, but within a more confined space. And of course the constant shoveling of snow, the great obstacle between the farm and the rest of the world, the pressure of the cold, and all those wintry things, in the end, that commit us to staying at home.

All around them, nothing but a solid white thickness, canceling the landscape, and a crunching underfoot with every step.

Norma and Spencer would sit in their dimly lit living room, staring out at the great void, the blank page, where only one or two tree trunks cut notches into the otherwise uniform whiteout. And the two of them wondered how they were going to come to grips with all this colorlessness.

When winter came to campus, you'd look out your window as snow covered the quad, then you'd go out and mingle your foggy breath with that of your fellows until you got to your classroom, a bit sweaty and out of breath from climbing the stairs in the overheated building, since you'd kept on your hat and scarf and down jacket. And once again, out the classroom windows, the spectacle of snow covering up the last traces of grass, erasing even the memory of green beneath the white compactness of accumulated flakes—though here and there, unexplainable bald spots where the snow wouldn't stick, something that was resisting the overwhelming majority of snowfall.

Do our thoughts also dig in for the winter, hibernating until the spring thaw, isn't there a seasonal slowdown to the way we look at the world, a sleepier behavior in general, as sound becomes muffled outside and even the sky freezes into place, suspended until further notice?

20

THE THRIFT STORE IS set back from the road on an empty lot whose only embellishment was a set of two red trash bins in the same poppy red as the store sign.

A little break from driving would do Donovan some good, to stretch his legs and move at a normal walking speed for a bit; besides, he might find a little knick-knack to bring Tom Lee.

You never know what you might come across in a thrift store, do you?

Browsing in one of these places is a little like deep-sea diving for eighteenth-century shipwrecks, pulling out objects corroded by time and salt water, which you inspect through your diver's mask.

A bazaar of sundries that had once served a purpose, now washed up onto these pathetic shelves where they bear witness to a bygone era that shoppers suspect they themselves once belonged to, seemingly foreign-looking objects, waiting to be desired.

In short, there's something poignantly poetic about thrift stores, and if you've never experienced the magic, now's your chance.

Donating their earnings to whatever cause they deem supportive of the general good, such as the protection of raptor species (which might not have immediately sprung to mind as a possibility), they store all manner of junk in large concrete storage sheds or other metallic structures, where you're likely to find just about anything, all sorted according to function and size.

You can walk through entire aisles of such objects, scanning whole series of teapots, coffee pots, and cups (mostly in mug format, tall and cylindrical, but some also seem to come from the Old World, porcelain teacups in faded rose patterns), a jumble of items that rustle with stories, whispering the names of the places they came from and what string of misadventures landed them in this place.

A dwarf in a cap, an earthenware cactus, clay rabbits with hollow backs that must have served some purpose, a pig in a top hat (don't blame me), geese with ribbons around their necks, two little earthenware girls in floppy bonnets sitting on a bench (again, it's not my fault), a tiny box with "My First Tooth" written across the lid, I swear I'm not making this up. On the other side of this same aisle, shallow bowls, glasses, nondescript containers of various sorts, nothing as eye-popping as the stuff on the opposite side (whose bestiary keeps adding members, polar bears, herons, it never ends), but which probably have quite a story to tell, like this tagine dish which, if it's an original, must have a considerable odyssey behind it (I come from far, far away, it would begin, and you'd be treated to scenic descriptions that I'll bet none of the others had ever heard), a hurricane lamp (did it just sit in the closet near the front door in the event of an electrical outage, or maybe it was taken down to the dunes, into the salty sea air, swinging from a solitary arm, and set between two or three friends smoking in the dark of night on a deserted beach, sharing their secrets), a plastic wall clock, round and flat, your standard-issue school clock, the ones you find in the cafeteria, but which would keep time just as well in your own kitchen, if that's what you like (you'd sit facing it, your hands folded on the plastic tablecloth, watching those domestic minutes tick by).

Everything in there has an Oliver Twist feel about it, pathetically wistful, clutching its wanderer's narrative for dear life.

And if some retreat into a disillusioned passiveness (a bit like those zoo animals that don't even attempt to make eye contact with you anymore, you who are making such an effort there on the other side of the cage, because they know how little they can expect from your feigned concern, how quickly you'll be on your way, since the only thing that interests you is the chance to prove your capacity to get a caged animal to distinguish you from among all the other visitors, think how rewarding it would be; instead you get the listless look of depressing reverie, staring into space, taking no interest whatsoever in your person, or anyone else's, the annihilating look of indifference), most are still hoping for a buyer, watching you as you roam the store (it must be so much nicer in your house than in this drafty shell of a place with piped-in music on a perpetual loop and the chilly ambiance of a third-tier retirement home).

Aren't you having a surge of tenderness for one of them, this sugar bowl, for instance, whose floral pattern has mostly faded by now, but whose handles are still yearning to be grasped? And look at the lid, topped with a raspberry, the better to lift it. If you poke your nose inside, you'll note that ineffable fragrance of musty cupboard, you know the one, a mix of dust and licorice tea, but you need only air it out a bit, rinse it with soapy water, and the stale smell will be gone, soon to be replaced by the odor of your own apartment and the bland smell of the overly refined sugar it will contain.

You might also stop and listen to the extended lamentation of a napkin ring that can't resign itself to bearing that name, whose painted letters are beginning to chip, and whose namesake is nowhere to be seen. Abandoned by this "Brad," whose dinner napkin it must have served to identify (since, as we all know, the only thing more repulsive than greasy stains that you yourself made on your checkered napkin—they're usually checkered, as a rule—is to find yourself wiping your mouth on somebody else's grease-stained napkin, something beyond disgusting for most of us), it sits there, desperate for some other Brad to pass by, your name isn't Brad by any chance, it asks you when you get within reading range of the lonely little napkin ring.

And not to be outdone, this trivet tells you what it feels like to have a scalding hot soup tureen plopped down on your belly (or even more painful, a casserole just out of the oven), it's not an easy life, but sitting here doing nothing is much worse, you can't imagine, and if it had hands to wring as it laid out its complaint, it would be wringing the heck out of them.

Every item in the shop is a tale of woe, a litany of abandonments and adoptions, of endless shunting from one house to the next, a different owner each time, only to end up huddled and shivering on these shelves as we look on; while some appear to be soliciting our sympathy, still believing in their powers of seduction, despite patches and cracks, others have clearly given up, all bashed in and broken, turned in on themselves like pathological introverts, not realizing that they still have a chance, because it's just like you to forgo the more able-bodied and fall for a poor wretch reliving its halcyon days that you'd love to revive. And you grab a few of these items no one wants, you hold them up, close to your eyes, lock gazes with them, something they're not at all accustomed to anymore, and they find consolation even in this unhoped-for attention.

Donovan is won over by an amateur oil painting, a scene of a cottage daubed onto plywood, intense blue sky, tall, uncut grass, the cottage seemingly abandoned, and a rocking chair on the porch, I believe.

There's obviously no reason to think he needs to bring something for Tom Lee. Between longtime friends, such niceties are almost inappropriate. You're more likely to bring a hospitality gift to someone you hardly know, as a show of good faith for that very reason, to acknowledge your appreciation of the complex offering they've extended by inviting you into their home, a token in exchange for the hours spent in their interior, fitting into their ways as best you can, sleeping in one of their beds, eating their home-cooked meals, pumping an ounce or two of their bath gel into your hand, clumsily getting water all over their bathroom floor, and the most intimate, perhaps the most touching of all, using their toilet paper; yes, there is practically a list of standard items guests are expected to present their hosts—flowers, potted or in a bouquet, a bottle of wine, some fine chocolates or pastries—any of these would do.

But some useless item of junk, that's an entirely different matter, and this piece of amateur artwork will look just great over the fireplace at his ranch, let's trust Donovan, who sets the painting on the checkout counter in front of the woman in a pink smock surrounded by displays of knickknacks, who doesn't seem terribly interested in knowing what he intends to do with it, as she stuffs the thing into a plastic bag while she carries on chatting with another woman, also in a smock, about her plans for the coming Saturday, how she intends to get plastered, how it'll piss off her boyfriend again, but what else is there to do on a Saturday night out here in the heartland, she asks her coworker, and she takes Donovan's five-dollar bill, Thank you, sir.

Outside, the light is softening, the shadows growing longer, the chain-link fencing around the lot casting a net over the only three vehicles parked there.

21

THERE'S ANOTHER STORY GOING around among the locals, and that's the one about Linda Burn's brother.

Linda Burn's brother is a big guy who has always done as he pleases, and what pleases him most is to do what doesn't necessarily please everyone else.

He'd never done anything but the opposite of what he was asked to do, from the earliest requests he can remember.

To illustrate, when he was only seven, his mother got sick and told him to watch his two little sisters, five and four years old (Norma and Linda, if you're following the family saga). So, would you believe that he took them out to the sheep pen and left them there with the animals, apparently not seeing any difference between sheep and his sisters, and then ran away from home for several days, the first of many such temporary disappearances, from which he would always come home in the end.

And every time he did, the father would give him a whipping to remember, but the threat of punishment was never great enough to deter him.

Linda Burn and her sister spent their childhood rocking to the rhythm of the prodigal son's comings and goings, in awe and fear of his freedom.

The father expressed his paternal love by greeting the son's return with these beatings, rather than the proverbial open arms and forgiveness, which he never deemed particularly useful in such cases. Any words of kindness directed at William Burn (this was the son's name, or if you prefer, Linda's brother's) would have seemed like a violation of his rule of tough love, however unconditional, toward the son, or toward the adult he would become, when he would awkwardly reproduce the father's features, the little bastard, an inferior copy of his dad, riddled with flaws, a second-rate imitation, blurry and lacking definition, so much like him but a more evasive, slighter, underachieving version.

That was William Burn in a nutshell, an ill-defined entity, always on the verge of vanishing, and who compensated for his lack of definition by surges of independence, disappearing for days at a time only to better reappear, redefined by what had been hounding him, out there in the underbrush or on the outskirts of cities where he'd hang out for days, discovering what he was all about, in the sand and dead weeds, and later, in the local bars, in pursuit of the fleeting phantom of his identity.

With this story of Linda Burn's brother, we might be over-speculating, but it's also possible, when you think about it, that William Burn, rough-and-tumble as described, might have passed through that little town, and assuming that he knew something about his sister Norma and her relationship with Spencer O'Johnson, and about his other sister Linda, including her recent misadventures with Tom Lee, which is perfectly plausible, since he did always come back, no matter how long the absence, and kept in touch with the family throughout it all, though his relationship with them was like a rubber band, stretched to its maximum length, then suddenly snapped back into shape when he would show up after a long hiatus and the family would re-aggregate into its friable yet definitive unit. So, as I was saying, it's altogether possible that he passed through this town, and that he became the inhabitants' principle informant in the matter.

It's in their interest to imply as much, at any rate, and it's what they're having you believe without coming out and saying so, preferring to keep things mysterious, serving up the old We Protect Our Sources line of argument.

As they tell it, William Burn has gone all craggy and chiseled, and this sculpted face of his turns out to be the answer to his self-definition issues, with all that frowning and wrinkling against the desiccating winds having etched permanent grooves into his skin, erasing what remained of his indecisiveness, the elusiveness that once characterized his facial features, and leaving in its place something more expressive that bears up under scrutiny.

It's no longer an unfinished face, but you might call it a haggard face, a witness to the trial-and-error nature of his self-discovery, tentative versions crossed out and replaced, only to be crossed out in turn, a thousand rough drafts that end up giving him the allure of a work in progress, the long, tattered manuscript that William Burn schleps from city to city.

For years, they fretted over William Burn, his unstable personality, his repeated attempts to run away from home, a youngster going down the wrong path, and people spoke his name with a mix of overt disapproval and altruistic concern. But when it became clear that he was just a good-for-nothing barfly who wandered from town to town, they stopped caring at all. He was no longer that troubled young man who could still make something of himself, even though such opportunities were dwindling, and most agreed that his future looked dim: no, he was a failure, and that's all there was to it, the votes were unanimous. You could be around him now with a clear conscience, he was just part of the local scenery, no one talked about him anymore behind his back, no one voiced any fear for his future, but just took him for what he was, William Burn, the itinerant drunk, and folks were even happy to see him, since his arrival always meant there'd be fresh material, which he'd impart in that slow nasal drone of his, as if he didn't realize what a gold mine of anecdotes he possessed.

Still, even though the folks in the little town near the ranch are grateful for the news that he spreads quite effortlessly by virtue of his roving lifestyle, gleaning and reporting stories as he moves from town to town, there's no denying that the mere mention of Linda's brother almost always spells trouble, nothing serious, more like a low rumble, the hissing of an evil wind, or something in people's eyes, the way they go muddy all of a sudden when they hear the name.

The very least you can say about William Burn is that he's the restless kind, and that's basically the thing folks just can't handle. Has it ever occurred to any of them, for instance, to complain about their one-horse town, which, to their mind, is as good a place to live as any? Burn's unwillingness to put down roots in one town or the other threatens them in a way they'd have trouble explaining, even more than his drunken boisterousness that does nothing but make them all itch for a fight. What is this mysterious knowledge, this higher calling (or this overwhelming incompetence of his that defeats all second guesses) that causes him to forgo the settled life in a town, any town, and prefer what can only be called a hobo's existence, which is clearly not a picnic? I mean, just look at him.

The most hostile among them is undoubtedly Earl Wilson, who blends the townsfolk's shared displeasure with a more personal grievance linked to some episode from the past that he often alludes to, but without any clarification.

Earl was a seasonal worker at Spencer's.

Spencer is really the type of guy who cares for nothing beyond his own self-interest. The notion that his seasonal workers might have lives of their own, with a past, memories, regrets, and for the more forward-looking among them, plans for the future, would simply never occur to him. They're not much more than tools that he consigns to the barn every evening to sleep. He hasn't a clue about the world that each of them carries around under his cap.

There's no mystery as far as Spencer is concerned: the farm is all about Norma and himself, who, though (temporarily) uncoupled by his extramarital escapades, will always come together again when he returns, which he inevitably does, and why wouldn't he, after all, since it all belongs to him; besides, those brief getaways serve only to purge his chronic existential dissatisfaction, but they're what make possible a peaceful coexistence with Norma, and isn't that what escapades are often for?

Spencer hires his seasonal workers pretty randomly, paying them for work done and caring little about who they are, where they're from, or what they look like, even when they might possess a physical appearance, a body mass index or musculature that seem incompatible with the job. He figures the guy has an idea about what he's getting into, and if he thinks he can handle the work, even with that build, then that's his business.

Which is why he rarely even glances in their direction, never looks them over with an eye toward their suitability, in fact he grants them no personal existence whatsoever: they are what they produce, and that's all there is to it. And I believe that if someone were to tell him that one of his hires was getting a little too close to Norma, he'd blow the guy's brains out before even considering the obvious fact that the guy had a body, and that he'd have to dispose of the mortal remains.

So every time Earl Wilson saw William Burn make an unexpected entrance into the local watering hole with that air of someone who'd never left town, and step up to the bar just like the regulars do, to the annoyed surprise of everyone present, Earl seemed to recollect a scene he witnessed a long while back.

What it has to do with William Burn, I'm not so sure, but since Spencer is his brother-in-law, maybe that's enough for Earl Wilson to make the connection.

He's also Norma's brother, Linda's too, and Earl would have had quite a bit to say about the two sisters, if he had so chosen.

But Earl has never talked about any of that, and every time he sees William Burn, he starts fiddling with his earlobe (pinching it between his thumb and index finger, twisting it every which way, like he was trying to reshape it), he wonders whether it might be a good time to speak up.

What they've managed to get out of Earl, once they've grilled him a little, is that the scene involved William Burn and Spencer O'Johnson.

A fight that he witnessed, maybe after a local dance, something that took place in some out-of-the-way spot, in an empty field, by the light of a half-moon that couldn't have cared less.

Earl saw things at a certain distance, impeded by a barbed hedge, with no intention of intervening.

Not at all impossible that he enjoyed the idea of the two of them going at each other like that in the moonlight, the punches and the pain, the mess they were making, rolling in the dew-drenched grass that would tear away and stick to their clothing streaked in what would have appeared red and green, were it not for the darkness that rendered the scene in black and white.

It would be an understatement to say that Earl didn't much care for Spencer, nor did he remember his time at the farm with any fondness. After all, Spencer was the guy who won the heart of Norma Burn, who, for someone like Earl, was the ultimate prize, the star he dared not even approach when she was still a girl, and who Spencer snatched up just like that, effortlessly, without experiencing those periods of bungled schemes, of trial and error, the uncertainty, the shyness, the despair of ever fulfilling the dream, then, in the end, the satisfaction of effort rewarded; no, it took him only one night, with an ease so disconcerting as to undermine everything Earl had ever believed.

As for William Burn, he was just a good-for-nothing hobo drunk that no one would trust further than they could toss, and Earl never buddied up to him.

Even for Norma, who was his sister, after all, even for her, he felt no reason to interfere, since Norma had seen fit to run off with Spencer while he, Earl, meant no more to her than an ant she might have crushed underfoot on her way home from a dance, arm in arm with Spencer, grinding it into the earth with the sole of her shoe.

And the ant slowly reemerged, a bit dazed, its little antennae shaking off the dust, its powdered body wounded and broken as it spat out tiny grains of sand that had lodged in its mouth, and it made an oath that it has kept to this day.

So, the two drunken bodies bathed in the half-moon's glow were tearing each other's guts out against the silhouette of a shriveled apple tree that lightning had struck the previous summer, and whose branches seemed frozen into a pose of helpless supplication, raised toward the sky that had rained down its wrath.

Did all this have anything to do with Linda, did William finally get it, had he seen something, seen Spencer making his moves? You're asking too much, I'm afraid, and Earl never said any more than what I've just told you, but just walked back, head down, mulling over a few notions that are his alone to know.

Despite this one mystery, overall, we've got the Burn clan pretty well figured out. There's a thumbnail sketch for each, the sisters, the brother-in-law, Spencer's father, the Burn brother, everyone's present and accounted for.

Now, if you were to take a photograph out of your pocket, right here, a picture of three children amidst a scenery of sand dunes, frozen in the frame as they rushed forward, Pompeii lava style, and if you were to tell me, pointing a confident finger in a way that made me want to believe you, that this one is William, immediately recognizable by his blurry, withdrawn look; and that one, with something slightly clumsy about her but stubbornly determined to join in the game, though her mind seems elsewhere, that one is, of course, Norma; and the youngest, there's no mistaking, having come into a world built without her, Linda, ordinarily loved and ordinarily envied by the two others, you can see her running along like her siblings in the friable, unstable sand, which she spits out, yuck!, using her hands to get it off her tongue, making matters worse, little pint-sized Linda, the same one who, years later—and something in her eyes seems to foreshadow it, hers being the only gaze of the three to look straight into the lens—would meet Tom Lee, spend a night with Elizabeth James, surrender her body to Rick, and finally set off once again; if you were to rummage through your things and pull out this seaside snapshot of children playing in the soft, friable sand, and you manage to convince me that William, Norma, and Linda Burn are the ones in the picture, when all three were just kids, all in the same frame that they seem to be trying to break out of as they run, well, all I could say is, wow, I'm impressed.

22

BACK IN THEIR COLLEGE days, Donovan also had a novel in progress.

It was about a young woman who meets a guy her age, I'm not sure how, in some state far from her hometown, but nothing happens between them despite a clear mutual attraction, either out of shyness, or laziness, uncertainty, misunderstandings, or blindness to their own desire, in other words an intricate interlacing of causes that would require endless hours to catalogue if you were ready to give it the attention it deserved (and Donovan seemed prepared to launch into just such an inventory). Then she moves away and he stays, each one back on his or her ground (two different-sized American cities, far apart and with very different weather), where they each seem to be living alone, without any romantic attachment (even though a part of the suspense depends on precisely that question, not only because there's a chance they haven't told each other everything, but that anything could happen at any moment). They begin corresponding, and readily admit that, among all the memories they enjoyed sharing, there is one missing. Which is why the novel was to be entitled *The Missing Memory*.

What's missing, of course, is their night of lovemaking. But once they've each agreed that they have been deprived of a certain memory, and each asks the other what they think it might be ("I know it might be dangerous to ask, but could it be the same one?"), when it comes time to actually fill in the blanks, so to speak, the best they can come up with is a prudish kiss in the moonlight. The boy evokes a field near his house

162

that would be perfect for a first embrace; and they proceed to conduct a little epistolary reverie on the subject (he asks her, if this were to take place where she's now living, is there a place she has in mind?), and they describe to each other the kind of scenery they think best suited to that moment when their lips first touch, lips that are, for the moment, hundreds of miles apart, a variable reverie with its ups and downs, its lulls and revivals, new turns of phrase that rekindle emotions that serve to celebrate, as one would a ritual, the missing memory and the prospect of its fulfillment.

But all that is more like the novel's prehistory (seriously, what do you think, Tom, a whole book made up of nothing but a series of scenic descriptions of places where they dream of getting it on, some from the girl's perspective, some from the boy's, a different one every time? I don't know, it seems to me that twelve landscape descriptions, for example, one section of the book for each, some really romantic, exactly what you'd expect, a fallen tree in a forest clearing, an area of undergrowth along Route 66, and the like, while others would be more off-beat, do you think that would work? And you'd be doing all this listing of tree species, all the precision talk of perspective and vanishing points, to get across the main point, which is their frustrated desire for that first kiss, the thing they long for with all their might, not knowing whether or not it will ever happen).

The real story starts when the girl decides to come back.

A year had gone by, shored up by those sporadic letters, vague promises to get back together, the logistical problems that had thus far prevented them from doing so (work schedules, travel costs . . .), bits of news, the easiest daily episodes to convey in writing, personal anthology entries nicely condensed, just to keep the other up to date on their doings (The time I saw a tapir, My weekend with friends, How mist was hanging over the lake yesterday, How much I'd like to walk along this river with you, etc.).

The clever thing would be to write it from the girl's point of
view, advised Tom Lee.

The sharp edge of the bench was making their butts hurt, and
the dampness had begun to creep up their shins. They passed
a single cigarette back and forth, with all the seriousness of
those who believed the tip glowing orange with each puff could
somehow keep them warm. They exhaled the smoke into the
American night, a noisy, propulsive sound, as if to make sure all
this were real, the smoke, the bench, and they themselves, this
midnight in the USA.

Still, Tom Lee wasn't altogether sure that it would make much
difference, when it came to the nature of the emotions involved,
desire, patience, uncertainty, and determination, but it's good
that you work on the girl's voice, don't you think? Since she's the
one who comes back, who travels all that way to see him again.
Makes sense, doesn't it?

So, in the end, Donovan's novel starts with the scene of the girl
on the plane on her way to hook back up with, let's call him,
Ben. And not only did it begin in the plane, but it was soon
obvious to Donovan that the whole novel (not a very long one,
mind you) had to be about only that, the trip back to reunite
with Ben, during which she would be recalling the time they'd
spent together the previous year, with all the little symptoms of
their budding but unfulfilled desire. The signs she'd been unable
to interpret, blinded as she was by her own inner turmoil,
whose emotional meaning became apparent to her only later
in a series of soulful revelations. She also recalled the letters
they'd exchanged over the months. But most especially, she'd be
looking forward to their reunion, picturing how it would unfold,
imagining an endless number of scenarios of that long-awaited
airport moment. And she endeavored to analyze everything she

felt about that idea, the joy and the fear that clashed in the pit of her stomach at that altitude, while outside the plane portholes, fantastical cloudscapes were unfurling their cottony scrolls.

And so it continued, descriptions of the sky, carpets of clouds so white they hurt your eyes, bizarre shapes ranging from the benign to the monstrous (some seemed to rise out of the undifferentiated mass the way sculpted figures emerge from rough blocks of stone, the maw of a dragon, the outline of a yeti, or whatnot), or commentary on the little world of the jet airliner, the carpet, the screens, the unlaced shoes, the sense of normalcy that takes over, thousands of feet in the air, inside the pressurized cabin, as she alternated between memories of her previous stay (all the overlooked significance that their correspondence had revisited and revived), and the nervous expectation of their imminent reuniting.

What mattered most in this midair interlude was to show that there wasn't only joy and fear in the heart of the female protagonist (nor only in Ben's, as he woke up at home, got out of bed, got dressed, had breakfast, got in the car and set off for the airport, negotiating everything differently that day, all those little familiar, concrete realities that made up his life, because he knew that he was going to see her, and that he was also a little scared of not measuring up; and from her seat on the plane, she imagined him getting dressed, fixing breakfast, sitting down to eat at his kitchen table with its plastic tablecloth covered in a pumpkin motif, all feverish inside at the idea that this thing they'd planned a thousand times, without ever knowing whether it would take place, was about to happen), not only joy and fear, as I was saying (by that, I mean all the fears triggered by this kind of situation, one's own as well as those bearing on the other's intentions, which may well have changed in the meantime, or which could change in the near future, once he

sees you again—will he still want you—since you're not quite
the person you were a year ago, not the one stored in memory,
revisited and remodeled, but another, exhausted by the trip,
complexion lusterless, eyes ringed in dark circles, clothing a
mass of wrinkles from so much sitting), not only that particular
kind of excitement, but also a certain feeling inside—and let's be
honest here—of erosion, of forgetting and indifference, almost,
despite the best efforts of your surge of joy, whose victory is by no
means guaranteed. Or was it a strategy, an unconscious defense
mechanism, this concomitant sense of joy and detachment,
this apathy that you felt looming, that you thought was already
present in low dosage, though not imperceptible, a form of
self-preservation in the event that the other greeted you in the
arrivals hall with a polite handshake (since his most recent letters
hadn't been quite as explicit as earlier ones when it came to those
first moments of their getting back together)? It was perfectly
possible, after all, that you'd hardly have gotten into the car,
your bag stowed in the trunk, having exchanged a perfunctory
hug at arrivals, absolutely possible that, before he even started
the car, staring straight ahead over the steering wheel into the
back of the parking garage, that he would tell you, reciting as if
from memory, that he'd promised himself he'd explain it all to
you, had been searching for the right words as he was driving
to the airport, so here's the thing, I've met somebody, I'm with
someone else now, I'm really happy to see you, but that's all, and
that's all there will be, it has to be all there is, and you're telling
him that a kiss is no big deal, that he owes you at least that, come
on, or maybe it'd be just the reverse, you'd sit back in your seat
and admit to yourself that this turn of events suits you just fine,
that you're not attracted to him at all anymore, that you can see
what it is about his physical presence that you don't like, what
you find alien about him, the thing about him that you don't
want to get so close to that your breath is mingling, and all the
rest.

The girl, sometimes with her nose pressed to the porthole as she gazed at the amazing cloud formations, sometimes more focused on the cabin's bustling activity, the busy stewardesses, the way each one had personalized her uniform by adding a touch all her own, her hairstyle, the way she tied her scarf, something about the way they all emanated a *je ne sais quoi* about their own love lives as they walked up and down the aisles, their ankles swollen from the cabin pressure, and back to our girl, other times, she would just sit back under her plaid blanket and stare at the seat in front of her, a neutral, gentle gaze, and begin screening her imaginary scenarios again, testing how she might feel about the prospect of an actual relationship with Ben (all those situations in which they would have to be interacting—reality implies a major expenditure of energy), and a kind of weariness would set in, originating in the notion that this trip had been decided months in advance (it's already an old thing), that the intervening period might have had the effect of dampening desire rather than stoking it, because her attention had been drawn to all sorts of other things that had nothing to do with Ben, distracting her from her goal, which was to meet back up, a prospect they had kept alive through their correspondence (and just then it occurs to her that Ben might not be the one she wants to see again, but instead I'll just take one example among many, that young Brazilian musician who, only a few weeks ago, spent a whole evening begging her to give him a chance, who seemed to have such a confident attitude toward pleasure (*Posso te fazer muito feliz*, I can make you very happy), so frenetically joyful, that maybe this is what she wanted now, rather than Ben's sweet shyness, she wished the plane were landing in Rio, where the musician would be waiting for her, his body shivering with single-minded, initiative-taking purpose, and where everything would fall into place with such ease).

The female protagonist's feelings, which Donovan felt lay at the very heart of the narrative, were not monolithic, far from it. And her location on a plane, as she reflects back on times spent with Ben and on what awaited her upon arrival, allowing her to conduct her reverie up in the sky, an incongruous place to be, if you think about it (personally, I've never been able to get used to the idea, and I cling to whatever there is in the plane that reminds me of life back on terra firma: the nubby texture of the carpeting absorbs my gaze that feigns interest in the intricate detailing of its color range and thickness, all the better to avoid looking out the windows at the frightening void, if you can even believe what you're seeing), the fact that she's sailing along above the clouds at such a vast distance from what's going on down below lends a gossamer haziness to her thoughts, like the texture of the clouds themselves through which the plane is speeding like a spinner's distaff ripping through the raw cotton it's processing.

There she was, in this enclosed, circumscribed cabin space, where all she could do was unbuckle every so often to stand up and stretch her legs in the aisle, or ask for another cup of coffee back in the service area where a couple of passengers were doing their isometric exercises, supposedly good for blood circulation, despite the extremely limited latitude for movement in such a narrow, confined place, where by the end everyone feels trapped, where your body is basically bound to a seat, secured by your safety belt; but at the same time she was rocketed into the vastness of the lower stratosphere, cruising along in the plane's predetermined flight pattern, watching the sky's grandiose spectacle through its tiny windows.

At first, it was all her little fears overwhelming her at once, joining forces to form one large mobile fear, a wavy mass of little fears in league with one another, marching through our protagonist's brain in a thundering procession. Her panic at the intensity of what was about to happen, at how inventive she would have to be in order to make these moments memorable and happy (would you even be capable of such a thing?); fear of not being the person he expected, of arriving with an altered face, a pudgier body, wearing rumpled clothing, as we said previously, fear that he might just throw in the towel when he sees you, that the sight of you might snuff out his desire. Or maybe yours, yes, what if it were you who didn't want him anymore, let's add that fear to the panic parade, the dread that it could be you, upon seeing him at the airport, who would wonder whether this trip had been such a great idea, and as he walks toward you, with that body that you'll have to hug, since that's what you came here for, after all, to fully embrace that body, to mingle yours with his, which fails to coincide with your memory of it, due to the little distortions induced by the way imagination operates, but also for more objective reasons, ones having to do with him and how he looks now (a little heavier, like you), something in his features that isn't quite the same, a subtle shift in his personality that took place over the previous year, a vibe you're having trouble recognizing, or a familiar one that has been extinguished, a general dispiritedness that has started to show, which you hadn't noticed the first time around, a sadness that has been fueled over the intervening period and is now taking up more room, inhabiting the space that was once so radiant (his carriage more encumbered, his gestures less precise, the accumulated effect of which is a more lumbering body walking toward you, further hobbled by his aura of gloom); and all that makes you feel suddenly trapped, and fear of entrapment gets added to your growing list of fears, this fear of being ambushed, because of vague promises that now bind you, because of the vast mural you'd painted together of what your reunion would look like, this future the two of you had so often detailed for yourselves that, now that it's coming true, is looking very different from what you'd imagined, so much so that you realize this isn't the role you want to play;

so what will you do if he takes you in his arms, what will you do, since the reunited couple scene won't work if you reject his advances, if, after this long plane trip, after his long drive to the airport, you murmur no, finally, no?

And then, gradually, you realize that all this is just a question of focus.

Here's what I mean.

All she had to do was to go back and recover the basic elements of their story together, to sift them out from all the alluvium that had built up over the past year, the accumulated sediment of anything foreign to their relationship, the desires and pleasures that may have flowed in and taken the place of theirs, just recover those essentials, separate them from the rest and reassemble them into their original whole.

All the emotion that had rushed through her right after her return home, the immutable memory palace where she wandered so happily, so endlessly, all the scenes she would visit and revisit, but which, over time, were overlaid with present events, the year's sum of actions and encounters that formed a necessarily opaque crust, all that could be revived and invigorated.

The fossilized memory of their time together, so stuck in the strata of the intervening months that she could hardly make it out anymore, not only reemerged, rose to the surface, but came back to life, what was once dead and practically gone was living and breathing once again. And from these revenants, desire could be rekindled.

So, in the end, with each passing hour of flight time, her worries evaporated, yielding to a brighter attitude toward what was to come.

She found she was able to picture more serenely the way the evening would unfold, a restaurant perhaps, a stop on the way to gaze at the moon, like all those moons they used to describe to each other in their letters, and a succession of kind, affectionate gestures, until they got to his place, where they'd sleep together in each other's arms, in the warm, damp sheets of his little bungalow, in the midst of the vast Oklahoma night.

Bottom line, said Tom Lee, sucking a last puff from his cigarette, the one closest to the filter, with the most tar and nicotine, and various other toxins, this novel of yours, you could have called it *Some Unfinished Business.*

In the end, the girl would get to the airport, where not only Ben would be waiting for her, but a whole committee, I don't know, people she made friends with the last time she was there, and she would greet them all with a casual hello, and would then catch sight of Ben, who was watching the scene from the sidelines, hands in his pockets, and she'd say to the little assembly: You'll have to excuse me, but I have some unfinished business with that little cowboy over there. And on that note, she'd leave with Ben, and they'd walk off together through the terminal and out to the parking lot.

A few years later, the book went to press under the title *The Missing Memory.* It sold fairly well, and Donovan was glad to run into Keith at a book signing event publicized in the local press, Wow, hey, how've you been, and they went for a drink at a bar across the street from the bookstore, Keith was doing great, actually.

He'd flipped through the book while he was waiting for Donovan to finish before heading to the bar, and read the last few pages. The story ended right when the plane landed, with the plane taxiing off the landing strip and into its dock, that interval when you're supposed to keep your seatbelt fastened, and all you see out the portholes are the grassy patches between the blacktopped lanes, and visible in the distance, the rectangular airport building that she hoped, if he wasn't running late, contained Ben.

23

We're getting close to the ranch now.

The sky is shifting, very slowly, nothing too noticeable yet, but tiny incontrovertible signs that it's that time of day when the hegemonic blue concedes defeat, each time as inevitable as the last, and yet each time a sight to behold.

There weren't always such gorgeous sunsets at the ranch, though. Sometimes night would fall all of a sudden, like an eye shutting. And when that happened, those two sitting together on the porch would feel like they'd been cheated. Like the night figured they weren't worth the trouble. Like there was no point going out of its way for the likes of them. And the landscape expired without warning, poisoned by the nocturnal inkiness. Tom Lee and Donovan felt like two minuscule bodies lost in the vastness of the surrounding land, insignificant entities breathing the humid air, crouching in their chairs, as if attempting to occupy the least possible space, in response to nature's verdict that they were unworthy of notice.

This was when Donovan would sometimes decide it was time to head back home, and he'd get in his car and drive into the moonless night, with only the twin beams of his headlights to assure him that there was something out there to drive on.

Tom Lee would walk him out to the car, aiming a flashlight at the sandy ground as they advanced, its round beam fighting a losing battle against the immensity of dark, cutting a moving hole in the blackness where bits of ground would appear to dance to the rhythm of their lazy gait.

Tom Lee was all but invisible, but Donovan recognized that step, the cadence at which his soles scraped the sand, his breathing too, and something he radiated, his body temperature perhaps; and this recognition sparked a feeling that resembled gratitude, not only for lighting the way forward to his station wagon, sparing him the blind grope, or for going to the trouble to get out of his chair and fetch the flashlight to walk him down to the vehicle; no, it was a more general thankfulness that made his ribcage expand, not so much for accompanying him down to the car as for simply existing, for breathing, for being a living body, the body of a friend whose mere proximity provided such relief, with whom he shared the experiences of the dewy air at nightfall, the sweet burn of bourbon, and the solitude of the prairie. This body, whose material presence he checks every so often with an open palm, a friendly pat on the back, and which served as his model for how best to sit under a porch overhang at dusk, how to walk on sandy ground, how to get around in the low, circumscribed, and intimate glow of a flashlight, whose reassuring beam at this precise moment in time is bringing it all back, yes, this present moment is powerful enough in itself to embrace all the others, to render them somehow co-present in the now, all the moments you've ever spent in each other's company, from your campus days until now, all rolled into one peacefully indistinct instant, the founding of a friendship.

At the end of every visit, even during daylight hours, Tom Lee walks Donovan to his car, the only difference being the sky's color and texture on any given day.

Sometimes, the send-off takes place beneath a flat, acrylic-blue sameness, so abstract as to cast their two silhouettes into high relief, as they stammer their goodbyes against this spotless backdrop. Two awkwardly approximate beings, poor souls whose countless flaws are woefully salient against the relentless monochrome.

On other occasions, it's the undulating clouds living out a precarious existence in their azure dwelling place. Their prettiness should provide a bucolic note to the scene, but instead injects something strangely poisonous, for these two parting friends have no business saying goodbye against such a cute, childlike background. The playful cotton puffs bathe in an idyllic blue, odiously deaf to the situation unfolding beneath them, as two men grapple somehow with those feelings we all experience when it comes time to part ways, and you know as well as I do that it's not just about how much you're going to miss that person as soon as the car pulls away, but that creeping, unspoken fear that flows silently underneath, having to do with the risk that any one separation, any given goodbye, and I might as well just go ahead and say it, might turn out to be the last.

And you can bet that when this is what they're feeling (and you have to deal with it every time, holding back the sled dogs of fear, pulling on those reins with all you've got despite their instinctual urge to forge ahead, as the painful ritual of departure is coming to a close), those adorable little balls of fluff floating by up there will feel like an insult to the depth of anguish you're experiencing down below.

Which is why you should never knock a cloudy day, those gray skies so compatible with the mood, their damp darkness infusing the scene with a sadness more appropriate to what is being played out at their feet.

It's just as possible that a highly unstable sky moving at breakneck speed will accompany the departure, and what you'd see in in such circumstances is not so much two fixed silhouettes, strengthened by the bonds friendship, standing firm against this backdrop in frenetic motion, but the way this instability would undermine them, as they stand there in silence, each enclosed in his own thoughts, and reveal what they have until now suppressed. For these high, mighty winds carry away anything unanchored, removing what little you have to call your own, leaving you naked and bereft. The two men would seek in vain to gather together the little events of their lives now scattered around them by the whipping wind, until the very memory of these life events is lost, leaving behind only the visceral experience of their disappearance.

We're driving slowly now in the gathering dusk that inevitably crashes the party of daylight's splendor, and whenever possible, completes its work with a dose of pyrotechnics, the pink transition phase and the poppy-colored stripes; yes, but as Mike used to say, when he would come join their little group on the campus green, the day dies a bloody death, and the deep reds that you all rhapsodize about, that's the blood of the dying day, the agony of massacred daylight, that's what dusk is so fiercely preying upon, stabbing it repeatedly until the final curtain falls, the black velvet curtain of night (and Mike would get up, chuckling to himself, and walk away toward the campus buildings, leaving Donovan and Tom alone on the little life raft of their bench, while the wind blew the grass into waves and the night fell unopposed).

We haven't got to that point yet, but we're in the earliest phases of transformation, still in those spine-tingling preparatory stages. Just a slight difference in the light, an almost imperceptible shift in the color of the sky.

Donovan parks the station wagon on the shoulder and gets out of the car, just to get the kinks out of his legs before the last few miles.

The landscape has gone amber, and trees are casting ever-lengthening shadows across the road and onto the plain.

On campus in late afternoon, the lateral rays of the setting sun laid down distended shadows of black walnut trees, deploying their gray tarpaulin across the grass in preparation for night.

The wind would occasionally carry strains of marching band rehearsals, while squirrels up in the branches made their little coughing noises at anything that moved.

Or they would go about their business in the grass, eating their walnuts, swift and sneaky, anxious or overjoyed, and sometimes they would bury nuts in places that made you wonder how they could ever remember where they were.

And the shadows continued to cloak the lawn, as plans for the evening started to take shape, beginning with a platter of nachos at some restaurant.

Donovan does a few stretches to loosen the tight spots in his joints.

He starts with some lower back muscle movements, hands on hips, rotating his torso, feels so good. Then the adductors, grabbing the knee and pulling it toward the chest, one leg then the other, as he gazes at the light that gilds the land.

Dusk permeates the visible universe, absorbing shape and thought.

We move gradually into night, with the same certainty as every other night, the same sense of dismay at daylight's pointless resistance.

Got to hit the road again soon, and you start thinking about all that again, the college years, Tom all alone on his ranch, and Jane, left behind in the cafeteria parking lot, who knows where she is now, Jane whom you'd love to see again sometime, and you tell yourself that maybe it might just happen, and you stand there a moment longer, your body immersed in the landscape, all that land under so much sky, thinking about that uncertain future possibility of being with Jane again, but also of the nearer, more likely future of getting together with Tom again, and you breathe in one more gulp of the outdoors before getting back in the car and driving on to what's next. Yes, here's to what's next.

CHRISTINE MONTALBETTI is an award-winning French novelist, essayist, critic and professor of literature at the University of Paris VIII.

JANE KUNTZ has translated ten works of fiction for Dalkey Archive, including *Talismano, Hotel Crystal, Everyday Life, Origin Unknown, Hoppla! 1 2 3*, and *Pigeon Post*. She holds a doctorate in Francophone Literature, and spent eighteen years in Tunisia. She now lives and works in Urbana, Illinois.

MICHAL AJVAZ, *The Golden Age.*
The Other City.
PIERRE ALBERT-BIROT, *Grabinoulor.*
YUZ ALESHKOVSKY, *Kangaroo.*
SVETLANA ALEXIEVICH, *Voices from Chernobyl.*
FELIPE ALFAU, *Chromos.*
Locos.
JOAO ALMINO, *Enigmas of Spring.*
IVAN ÂNGELO, *The Celebration.*
The Tower of Glass.
ANTÓNIO LOBO ANTUNES, *Knowledge of Hell.*
The Splendor of Portugal.
ALAIN ARIAS-MISSON, *Theatre of Incest.*
JOHN ASHBERY & JAMES SCHUYLER, *A Nest of Ninnies.*
GABRIELA AVIGUR-ROTEM, *Heatwave and Crazy Birds.*
DJUNA BARNES, *Ladies Almanack.*
Ryder.
JOHN BARTH, *Letters.*
Sabbatical.
Collected Stories.
DONALD BARTHELME, *The King.*
Paradise.
SVETISLAV BASARA, *Chinese Letter.*
Fata Morgana.
In Search of the Grail.
MIQUEL BAUÇÀ, *The Siege in the Room.*
RENÉ BELLETTO, *Dying.*
MAREK BIENCZYK, *Transparency.*
ANDREI BITOV, *Pushkin House.*
ANDREJ BLATNIK, *You Do Understand.*
Law of Desire.
LOUIS PAUL BOON, *Chapel Road.*
My Little War.
Summer in Termuren.
ROGER BOYLAN, *Killoyle.*
IGNÁCIO DE LOYOLA BRANDÃO, *Anonymous Celebrity.*
Zero.
BRIGID BROPHY, *In Transit.*
The Prancing Novelist.

GABRIELLE BURTON, *Heartbreak Hotel.*
MICHEL BUTOR, *Degrees.*
Mobile.
G. CABRERA INFANTE, *Infante's Inferno.*
Three Trapped Tigers.
JULIETA CAMPOS, *The Fear of Losing Eurydice.*
ANNE CARSON, *Eros the Bittersweet.*
ORLY CASTEL-BLOOM, *Dolly City.*
LOUIS-FERDINAND CÉLINE, *North.*
Conversations with Professor Y.
London Bridge.
HUGO CHARTERIS, *The Tide Is Right.*
ERIC CHEVILLARD, *Demolishing Nisard.*
The Author and Me.
MARC CHOLODENKO, *Mordechai Schamz.*
EMILY HOLMES COLEMAN, *The Shutter of Snow.*
ERIC CHEVILLARD, *The Author and Me.*
LUIS CHITARRONI, *The No Variations.*
CH'OE YUN, *Mannequin.*
ROBERT COOVER, *A Night at the Movies.*
STANLEY CRAWFORD, *Log of the S.S. The Mrs Unguentine.*
Some Instructions to My Wife.
RALPH CUSACK, *Cadenza.*
NICHOLAS DELBANCO, *Sherbrookes.*
The Count of Concord.
NIGEL DENNIS, *Cards of Identity.*
PETER DIMOCK, *A Short Rhetoric for Leaving the Family.*
ARIEL DORFMAN, *Konfidenz.*
COLEMAN DOWELL, *Island People.*
Too Much Flesh and Jabez.
RIKKI DUCORNET, *Phosphor in Dreamland.*
The Complete Butcher's Tales.
RIKKI DUCORNET (cont.), *The Jade Cabinet.*
The Fountains of Neptune.
WILLIAM EASTLAKE, *Castle Keep.*
Lyric of the Circle Heart.
JEAN ECHENOZ, *Chopin's Move.*

STANLEY ELKIN, *A Bad Man*.
The Dick Gibson Show.
The Franchiser.

FRANÇOIS EMMANUEL, *Invitation to a Voyage*.

SALVADOR ESPRIU, *Ariadne in the Grotesque Labyrinth*.

LESLIE A. FIEDLER, *Love and Death in the American Novel*.

JUAN FILLOY, *Op Oloop*.

GUSTAVE FLAUBERT, *Bouvard and Pécuchet*.

JON FOSSE, *Aliss at the Fire*.
Melancholy.
Trilogy.

FORD MADOX FORD, *The March of Literature*.

MAX FRISCH, *I'm Not Stiller*.
Man in the Holocene.

CARLOS FUENTES, *Christopher Unborn*.
Distant Relations.
Terra Nostra.
Where the Air Is Clear.
Nietzsche on His Balcony.

WILLIAM GADDIS, JR., *The Recognitions*.
JR.

JANICE GALLOWAY, *Foreign Parts*.
The Trick Is to Keep Breathing.

WILLIAM H. GASS, *Life Sentences*.
The Tunnel.
The World Within the Word.
Willie Masters' Lonesome Wife.

GÉRARD GAVARRY, *Hoppla! 1 2 3*.

ETIENNE GILSON, *The Arts of the Beautiful*.
Forms and Substances in the Arts.

C. S. GISCOMBE, *Giscome Road*.
Here.

DOUGLAS GLOVER, *Bad News of the Heart*.

WITOLD GOMBROWICZ, *A Kind of Testament*.

PAULO EMÍLIO SALES GOMES, *P's Three Women*.

GEORGI GOSPODINOV, *Natural Novel*.

JUAN GOYTISOLO, *Juan the Landless*.
Makbara.
Marks of Identity.

JACK GREEN, *Fire the Bastards!*

JIŘÍ GRUŠA, *The Questionnaire*.

MELA HARTWIG, *Am I a Redundant Human Being?*

JOHN HAWKES, *The Passion Artist*.
Whistlejacket.

ELIZABETH HEIGHWAY, ED.,
Contemporary Georgian Fiction.

AIDAN HIGGINS, *Balcony of Europe*.
Blind Man's Bluff.
Bornholm Night-Ferry.
Langrishe, Go Down.
Scenes from a Receding Past.

ALDOUS HUXLEY, *Antic Hay*.
Point Counter Point.
Those Barren Leaves.
Time Must Have a Stop.

JANG JUNG-IL, *When Adam Opens His Eyes*

DRAGO JANČAR, *The Tree with No Name*.
I Saw Her That Night.
Galley Slave.

MIKHEIL JAVAKHISHVILI, *Kvachi*.

GERT JONKE, *The Distant Sound*.
Homage to Czerny.
The System of Vienna.

JACQUES JOUET, *Mountain R*.
Savage.
Upstaged.

JUNG YOUNG-MOON, *A Contrived World*.

MIEKO KANAI, *The Word Book*.

YORAM KANIUK, *Life on Sandpaper*.

ZURAB KARUMIDZE, *Dagny*.

PABLO KATCHADJIAN, *What to Do*.

JOHN KELLY, *From Out of the City*.

HUGH KENNER, *Flaubert, Joyce and Beckett: The Stoic Comedians*.
Joyce's Voices.

DANILO KIŠ, *The Attic*.
The Lute and the Scars.
Psalm 44.
A Tomb for Boris Davidovich.

ANITA KONKKA, *A Fool's Paradise*.

GEORGE KONRÁD, *The City Builder.*

TADEUSZ KONWICKI, *A Minor Apocalypse.*
The Polish Complex.

ELAINE KRAF, *The Princess of 72nd Street.*

JIM KRUSOE, *Iceland.*

AYSE KULIN, *Farewell: A Mansion in Occupied Istanbul.*

EMILIO LASCANO TEGUI, *On Elegance While Sleeping.*

ERIC LAURRENT, *Do Not Touch.*

VIOLETTE LEDUC, *La Bâtarde.*

LEE KI-HO, *At Least We Can Apologize.*

EDOUARD LEVÉ, *Autoportrait.*
Suicide.

MARIO LEVI, *Istanbul Was a Fairy Tale.*

DEBORAH LEVY, *Billy and Girl.*

JOSÉ LEZAMA LIMA, *Paradiso.*

OSMAN LINS, *Avalovara.*
The Queen of the Prisons of Greece.

ALF MACLOCHLAINN, *Out of Focus.*
Past Habitual.

RON LOEWINSOHN, *Magnetic Field(s).*

YURI LOTMAN, *Non-Memoirs.*

D. KEITH MANO, *Take Five.*

MINA LOY, *Stories and Essays of Mina Loy.*

MICHELINE AHARONIAN MARCOM, *The Mirror in the Well.*

BEN MARCUS, *The Age of Wire and String.*

WALLACE MARKFIELD, *Teitlebaum's Window.*
To an Early Grave.

DAVID MARKSON, *Reader's Block.*
Wittgenstein's Mistress.

CAROLE MASO, *AVA.*

HISAKI MATSUURA, *Triangle.*

LADISLAV MATEJKA & KRYSTYNA POMORSKA, EDS., *Readings in Russian Poetics: Formalist & Structuralist Views.*

HARRY MATHEWS, *Cigarettes.*
The Conversions.
The Human Country.
The Journalist.
My Life in CIA.

Singular Pleasures.
The Sinking of the Odradek.
Stadium.
Tlooth.

JOSEPH MCELROY, *Night Soul and Other Stories.*

ABDELWAHAB MEDDEB, *Talismano.*

GERHARD MEIER, *Isle of the Dead.*

HERMAN MELVILLE, *The Confidence-Man.*

AMANDA MICHALOPOULOU, *I'd Like.*

STEVEN MILLHAUSER, *The Barnum Museum.*
In the Penny Arcade.

RALPH J. MILLS, JR., *Essays on Poetry.*

CHRISTINE MONTALBETTI, *The Origin of Man.*
Western.

NICHOLAS MOSLEY, *Accident.*
Assassins.
Catastrophe Practice.
Hopeful Monsters.
Imago Bird.
Natalie Natalia.
Serpent.

WARREN MOTTE, *Fiction Now: The French Novel in the 21st Century.*
Oulipo: A Primer of Potential Literature.

GERALD MURNANE, *Barley Patch.*
Inland.

YVES NAVARRE, *Our Share of Time.*
Sweet Tooth.

DOROTHY NELSON, *In Night's City.*
Tar and Feathers.

WILFRIDO D. NOLLEDO, *But for the Lovers.*

BORIS A. NOVAK, *The Master of Insomnia.*

FLANN O'BRIEN, *At Swim-Two-Birds.*
The Best of Myles.
The Dalkey Archive.
The Hard Life.
The Poor Mouth.
The Third Policeman.

CLAUDE OLLIER, *The Mise-en-Scène.*
Wert and the Life Without End.

PATRIK OUŘEDNÍK, *Europeana.*
The Opportune Moment, 1855.

BORIS PAHOR, *Necropolis.*

FERNANDO DEL PASO, *News from the Empire.*
Palinuro of Mexico.

ROBERT PINGET, *The Inquisitory.*
Mahu or The Material.
Trio.

MANUEL PUIG, *Betrayed by Rita Hayworth.*
The Buenos Aires Affair.
Heartbreak Tango.

RAYMOND QUENEAU, *The Last Days.*
Odile.
Pierrot Mon Ami.
Saint Glinglin.

ANN QUIN, *Berg.*
Passages.
Three.
Tripticks.

ISHMAEL REED, *The Free-Lance Pallbearers.*
The Last Days of Louisiana Red.
Ishmael Reed: The Plays.
Juice!
The Terrible Threes.
The Terrible Twos.
Yellow Back Radio Broke-Down.

RAINER MARIA RILKE,
The Notebooks of Malte Laurids Brigge.

JULIÁN RÍOS, *The House of Ulysses.*
Larva: A Midsummer Night's Babel.
Poundemonium.

ALAIN ROBBE-GRILLET, *Project for a Revolution in New York.*
A Sentimental Novel.

AUGUSTO ROA BASTOS, *I the Supreme.*

DANIËL ROBBERECHTS, *Arriving in Avignon.*

JEAN ROLIN, *The Explosion of the Radiator Hose.*

OLIVIER ROLIN, *Hotel Crystal.*

ALIX CLEO ROUBAUD, *Alix's Journal.*

JACQUES ROUBAUD, *The Form of a City Changes Faster, Alas, Than the Human Heart.*

The Great Fire of London.
Hortense in Exile.
Hortense Is Abducted.
Mathematics: The Plurality of Worlds of Lewis.
Some Thing Black.

RAYMOND ROUSSEL, *Impressions of Africa.*

VEDRANA RUDAN, *Night.*

GERMAN SADULAEV, *The Maya Pill.*

TOMAŽ ŠALAMUN, *Soy Realidad.*

LYDIE SALVAYRE, *The Company of Ghosts.*

LUIS RAFAEL SÁNCHEZ, *Macho Camacho's Beat.*

SEVERO SARDUY, *Cobra & Maitreya.*

NATHALIE SARRAUTE, *Do You Hear Them?*
Martereau.
The Planetarium.

STIG SÆTERBAKKEN, *Siamese.*
Self-Control.
Through the Night.

ARNO SCHMIDT, *Collected Novellas.*
Collected Stories.
Nobodaddy's Children.
Two Novels.

ASAF SCHURR, *Motti.*

GAIL SCOTT, *My Paris.*

JUNE AKERS SEESE,
Is This What Other Women Feel Too?

BERNARD SHARE, *Inish.*
Transit.

VIKTOR SHKLOVSKY, *Bowstring.*
Literature and Cinematography.
Theory of Prose.
Third Factory.
Zoo, or Letters Not about Love.

PIERRE SINIAC, *The Collaborators.*

KJERSTI A. SKOMSVOLD,
The Faster I Walk, the Smaller I Am.

JOSEF ŠKVORECKÝ, *The Engineer of Human Souls.*

GILBERT SORRENTINO, *Aberration of Starlight.*
Blue Pastoral.
Crystal Vision.

Imaginative Qualities of Actual Things.
Mulligan Stew.
Red the Fiend.
Steelwork.
Under the Shadow.
ANDRZEJ STASIUK, *Dukla.*
Fado.
GERTRUDE STEIN, *The Making of Americans.*
A Novel of Thank You.
PIOTR SZEWC, *Annihilation.*
GONÇALO M. TAVARES, *A Man: Klaus Klump.*
Jerusalem.
Learning to Pray in the Age of Technique.
LUCIAN DAN TEODOROVICI, *Our Circus Presents . . .*
NIKANOR TERATOLOGEN, *Assisted Living.*
STEFAN THEMERSON, *Hobson's Island.*
The Mystery of the Sardine.
Tom Harris.
JOHN TOOMEY, *Sleepwalker.*
Huddleston Road.
Slipping.
DUMITRU TSEPENEAG, *Hotel Europa.*
The Necessary Marriage.
Pigeon Post.
Vain Art of the Fugue.
La Belle Roumaine.
Waiting: Stories.
ESTHER TUSQUETS, *Stranded.*
DUBRAVKA UGRESIC, *Lend Me Your Character.*
Thank You for Not Reading.
TOR ULVEN, *Replacement.*
MATI UNT, *Brecht at Night.*
Diary of a Blood Donor.
Things in the Night.
ÁLVARO URIBE & OLIVIA SEARS, EDS., *Best of Contemporary Mexican Fiction.*
ELOY URROZ, *Friction.*
The Obstacles.
LUISA VALENZUELA, *Dark Desires and the Others.*
He Who Searches.

PAUL VERHAEGHEN, *Omega Minor.*
BORIS VIAN, *Heartsnatcher.*
TOOMAS VINT, *An Unending Landscape.*
ORNELA VORPSI, *The Country Where No One Ever Dies.*
AUSTRYN WAINHOUSE, *Hedyphagetica.*
MARKUS WERNER, *Cold Shoulder.*
Zundel's Exit.
CURTIS WHITE, *The Idea of Home.*
Memories of My Father Watching TV.
Requiem.
DIANE WILLIAMS,
Excitability: Selected Stories.
DOUGLAS WOOLF, *Wall to Wall.*
Ya! & John-Juan.
JAY WRIGHT, *Polynomials and Pollen.*
The Presentable Art of Reading Absence.
PHILIP WYLIE, *Generation of Vipers.*
MARGUERITE YOUNG, *Angel in the Forest.*
Miss MacIntosh, My Darling.
REYOUNG, *Unbabbling.*
ZORAN ŽIVKOVIĆ , *Hidden Camera.*
LOUIS ZUKOFSKY, *Collected Fiction.*
VITOMIL ZUPAN, *Minuet for Guitar.*
SCOTT ZWIREN, *God Head.*

AND MORE . . .